FOG CITY
FRAUD

D0792570

PETER RALPH

Typesetting and layout by WorkingType Design

Chapter 1

I WONDERED WHAT TOBY Evert's last thoughts were as he fell from the sixteenth floor of San Francisco's Mercantile Building. Had the shock of the bullet killed him when it ripped his shoulder apart, or was he still alive when he plummeted to the unforgiving pavement? Why had he forced our receptionist out onto the ledge with a knife at her throat? I didn't know much about him other than that he was a client of the firm. San Francisco cop Lieutenant Reid Rafter and I had convinced Evert to let Kirsty go. I'd spoken to him on the ledge, and he seemed a regular guy. He was in his early fifties with a cherubic friendly face, bald and genuinely remorseful. Before I went out the window, Rafter told me that Evert had been employed by the same engineering company for twenty years, was married, and had a twenty-four-year-old daughter. I knew he was no killer.

He'd done the wrong thing, no doubt about that, but what had driven an apparent solid citizen to barge into a professional office and take a young girl hostage? He'd been fuming when he grabbed Kirsty, but, within ten minutes of forcing her out onto the ledge, he'd agreed to let her go. He had even tried to help her back to the open window. What had made this seemingly quiet family man snap? What secrets had died with him? I hadn't known him, but I hoped the shock of the bullet had killed him. The alternative was too horrific to think about. God, it wasn't as if I hadn't already seen enough violent death.

I had been in my cubicle when I heard Kirsty scream and had raced down the corridor to find the reception area in chaos. Evert was standing behind the marble counter pressing a chef's knife against Kirsty's throat. He was shouting, "I want my money. You stole my money. Where's that slimy bastard, Eisler?" His eyes were rolling wildly, and he shook his head trying to flick the sweat off his spectacles. Kirsty was stark white, tears ran down her face, and she was shaking uncontrollably. I could hear the door to the stairwell being opened and closed as clients and staff clattered down the stairs shrieking. Ten or so staff who had remained were on the other side of the counter. Some of them were trying to calm Evert down and asking him to let Kirsty go. The trouble was they were all talking at the same time, and Evert's eyes were darting from one to another without focusing. Paul Wiese was the only senior manager in the group, and he looked like he wished that he had escaped with the others. The situation was grim, but I'd been in far worse, and I knew someone had to take charge or Evert might do something stupid and deadly. The stumbling block was that I was at the bottom of the firm's pecking order, and that's the way I liked it. The last thing I wanted to do was draw attention to myself, but I knew I had no choice. "Sir," I said in a deep firm voice, "whatever your concerns are, I know we can sort them out. You don't want to do anything stupid, so please put the knife down. I'm sure we can resolve your problems. There's no need for this."

"A baby-faced kid with a deep voice. Who are you?" Evert barked.

"Josh Kennelly, Sir. Please, if you just put the knife down and let Kirsty go, I'm sure we can resolve your problems amicably."

I wasn't a trained negotiator and had clearly used the wrong words. "They're not my problems!" Evert shouted, pressing the knife harder against Kirsty's throat. "My problems. They're your problems. You slimy bastards call yourselves investment advisers when you're no more than robbers. Your boss stole more than three million dollars from me. Should that be my problem, Joshy?"

"I'm sorry," I said, edging closer to the counter. "What can I do to make you put that knife down?"

"Nothing! And if you get any closer I'll slit her throat. Don't think I won't. Now back off."

"Yes, Sir."

I was watching Evert like a hawk, and, when he glanced over at the window, I instantly knew what he was thinking.

"I want the reception area cleared," he said, and when no one moved, he shouted, "Get out! Get out now. Not you, Joshy. You stay."

Employees fell over themselves trying to get out. I watched Paul Wiese run to the elevators, while others took the stairs. I knew police negotiators would be racing to the scene and that I had to stall Evert at all costs. "You know my name. What's yours?"

"You don't know? Eisler told me I was one of your firm's major clients. Lying bastard. I'm Tobias Evert, but enough talk. Get over there and open that window."

He had relaxed the knife a little and Kirsty gurgled, "Plea–please le–let me go. I did–didn't do any–anything to you."

"You don't want to hurt Kirsty, Mr. Evert. Why don't you let her go? I'll take her place. You can put the knife to my throat, and I promise I won't try and get away."

I'd pressed the wrong buttons again. "Do you think I'm a fool, Joshy?" Evert shouted. "Your bosses do. Now get over there, open the window, and get out of my way."

"You don't want to do th–"

"Now!"

I walked slowly toward the window with Evert following and pushing Kirsty in front of him. I pretended I couldn't undo the latch, and when I turned, Evert was only two yards behind me. "Don't play games, Joshy," he snapped, "or I'll cut her throat right now. Open the window and then back off out of the way. I'm through playing games."

Where are the cops? Where are they? "You don't want to do this, Mr. Evert. Kirsty's right. She hasn't done anything to hurt you. She doesn't deserve this."

As I opened the window a gust of wind sent papers and magazines flying everywhere. Evert, again, shouted at me to get away from the window. I watched on helplessly as he edged out onto the ledge. "Don't struggle," he growled at Kirsty, "or I won't be able to hold you."

Five minutes later, half a dozen cops charged out of the elevator. I was still at the window trying to talk sense into Evert and begging Kirsty to keep calm. She had stopped struggling, and Evert was holding her like a limp rag doll.

I felt a hand on my shoulder, and a fortyish policeman said, "I'm Lieutenant Rafter, and this is Officer Vicki Enright. Paul Wiese told us you were still up here, Josh. What's the lunatic want?"

I frowned. "He's not a lunatic, and I don't think he's dangerous. He has some misconceptions about the firm. I guess his investments are underperforming and he's blaming us. He demanded to see our CEO, Simon Eisler, but I don't think he's in the office."

"Ah, so you don't think he's crazy? Where was it you majored in Psychology? Yale, Harvard, Stanford?" Rafter sneered.

I ignored Rafter and instead looked out the window and said, "You don't want to do this, Mr. Evert. Why don't you edge back in?"

Before Evert could respond, Rafter shoved me out the way and said, "Mr. Evert, my name's Reid Rafter. I'm a police negotiator. Why don't you tell me what you want?"

"You can't help me, Mr. Rafter. You can't get my money back."

"Call me Reid, Mr. Evert. Things are never as bad as they first seem. Why don't you come inside, and we can talk about it? You don't want your loved ones seeing you on television like this, do you?"

As I looked down on California Street, two police vans screeched to a halt and heavily armed police poured out the rear doors. "What's going on, Officer Enright?" I asked.

"Vicki," she said. "SWAT."

"SWAT?" Are you mad? What can they do? If they shoot Evert, Kirsty's dead. It sounds like the inmates are running the asylum at SFPD, and your boss has the audacity to talk about lunatics."

"Standard procedure," Enright replied.

Chapter 2

RAFTER WAS BETTER AT his job than I had given him credit for. My gut was rarely wrong, but in this instance, I was glad it was. Evert and Kirsty were on the ledge about three to four yards from the window when the desperate man decided he had had enough. On reflection, it may have had nothing to do with Rafter. The wind had sprung up and was whistling around the high-rises, and the rain was just starting to spit. As if to confirm my thoughts I heard Evert say, "I want to come in, but my feet won't move. What am I going to do?"

"I'm going to die," Kirsty screamed, and tears streamed down her face.

"Stop wriggling," Evert said. "If you wriggle, I can't hold you."

"Hold on," Rafter said, "we'll have someone here to help you get inside soon."

There was a constant din from the walkie-talkies, cell phones, and laptops in the background. The thumping of the television stations' helicopters above the building made it worse. Officer Enright was only a yard away from me, and I could hardly hear her. The officer in charge of the SWAT team had a loud, raucous voice that drowned out other conversations. A cop standing a few yards behind me told him that Lieutenant Rafter had the situation under control but not to stand down yet. Another cop was on his cell phone shouting, "We urgently need a team to go out on the ledge to bring the perp and his hostage inside."

"Jesus, Vicki," I yelled, "there are hundreds of cops, and you didn't think to bring anyone who can go out on the ledge? In another fifteen minutes, it's going to be too wet to get out there. What were you thinking?"

"There aren't hundreds, and we didn't know they were on the ledge until we got out of the elevators. We called for assistance as soon as we found out."

Rafter turned around abruptly and said, "Stay out of it, smartass. We know what we're doing. Vicki, what did you find out about the perp?"

"Happily married for nearly thirty years, one child, Georgie, in her early twenties, lives in a nice house in Sausalito. Doesn't have a record."

"He's harmless." I butted in. "Something caused him to snap, but it's totally out of character. I can bring them in. It's not a problem."

"I told you to keep your nose out of it. You can help by keeping out of our way."

"The ledge is only damp now. In ten minutes, it'll be saturated. You'll never get them in," I said, kicking off my shoes and socks. "Get out of my way, Lieutenant."

Rafter's big body blocked my access to the window, and he shouted, "Butt out, Josh, and let us do our job. Vicki, get him out of the way."

"If I don't go out there now, it'll be too late. Do you want two deaths on your conscience, Lieutenant?"

Rafter was about to snap at me again when the window shook with the force of the wind. "I'll probably lose my job over this, but okay, get out there and for Chrissake, don't kill yourself," he said.

As I went out the window, there were three television helicopters immediately above me, and I cursed. If I were lucky, the fog would be too thick for their cameras.

An hour later, I sat in one of Summit's interview rooms with Vicki Enright. It was a small, glass-faced office with just a coffee table and three chairs, and of course, a rack filled with investment brochures. Officer Enright closed the drapes to provide us with a modicum of privacy.

I felt disappointed and was sad that a good man who had temporarily lost his way had been needlessly killed. Vicki made me a cup of coffee and spoke soothingly as we listened to what sounded like an army of police across the corridor examining the receptionist's area where the incident first began. I didn't say a word, and I knew she thought I was in shock. I wasn't. It was another ten minutes before Rafter barged through the door, and before he could speak, I asked him how Kirsty was.

"Poor kid. She's in the hospital, severely traumatized and under heavy sedation. It's going to be a long time before she psychologically recovers, if ever. You showed a lot of courage going out on that ledge, young man. Did Evert say why he took Kirsty hostage?"

"You heard him. He was after money and wanted to see our CEO, Simon Eisler. He got angry and lost it when Kirsty told him that Eisler wasn't available because he was in the Midwest."

"But he's not. He's in reception being interviewed."

I held my hands out, palms up. "I don't know, Lieutenant. Maybe Mr. Eisler was too busy to see him and told Kirsty to say he was in the Midwest."

Rafter put a gnarled hand up to his wrinkled forehead as if

in deep thought. "Did Evert say why he specifically wanted to see Eisler?"

"Something about his investments and being cheated," I replied, "but you can take that with a grain of salt."

"Why do you say that?"

"Every financial adviser has disgruntled clients. Why did your guys shoot him? Kirsty was safe, and I just about had him through the window."

"I dunno. One of the SWAT team must have seen him raise the knife and fired. There will be a full investigation."

"I'm sure that'll be comforting for his wife knowing that some trigger-happy cop's gonna get a rap over the knuckles for killing her husband. Real comforting!"

"You've got an attitude for one so young, Josh. What part of the south are you from?"

"A small town in Texas, Floydada, but I haven't been there for more than three months in the past six years. I thought I'd lost the accent. Oh, and I'm not that young."

Rafter smirked. "What are you? Twenty, twenty-one?"

I felt the color rush to my face. "I'm twenty-nine."

"Far out. You've got a baby face and don't even look like you shave. Jeez, Vicki, he says he's the same age as you. Do you believe him?"

"I wish I had his genes," Vicki replied, staring at me.

I'd taken crap like this most of my adult life and had half a dozen standard responses. "Lieutenant, you've got sunken jowls, you're overweight, your eyes are droopy, and you've got rapidly receding gray hair. You could easily pass for the wrong side of fifty, but I'm guessing early forties and a life filled with stress. How's that?"

Vicki put a hand over her mouth to muffle a laugh.

"You've got a smart mouth," Rafter said. "What do you do at Summit?"

"I prepare clients' tax returns."

"Do you advise on investments?"

"Never."

"What do you know about Mr. Evert's investments?"

"Nothing. You'll have to ask Mr. Eisler about them."

"We'll do that. In the meantime, we better get you to the hospital."

"I'm okay. I cleaned up. I've got a bit of blood spatter on my shirt. That's all. I'm fine."

"You might think you are, but you're going to have flashbacks and nightmares for years. Take it from me, you're going to need counseling, and the faster it starts, the better."

"Lieutenant, I don't need counseling."

"I don't care what you want, tough guy. You're going to the hospital to get checked out. Vicki will take you. Oh, here's my card. If you think of anything you haven't told us, call me. And don't forget, when the hospital clears you, you'll have to come in and make a statement."

I stood up pushing the chair into the wall behind me. "All right, let's get the bloody hospital over with."

The reception area was overflowing with police interviewing employees, taking photos, marking areas with chalk and taking measurements. Simon Eisler and his PA stood inches apart in the corner, whispering and looking around furtively.

Chapter 3

THERE WERE MORE COPS in the building's foyer, and the doors were locked. Vicki got one of them to open a side door. I felt a gust of cold air and prayed that the mist and light rain had hidden my involvement in the tragedy from the prying television cameras. California Street was still sealed off, and cable cars were backed up on both sides of the block. There was a forensic team examining the pavement where Evert had landed, and an ambulance was parked adjacent to the curb. Vicki took my arm and steered me toward the ambulance.

"I don't need an ambulance," I said.

"It's protocol," she responded. "Get in."

"You're not coming with me when I see the doctor."

"I didn't expect to. I'll be in the waiting room."

The entrance to the Jimmy Carter Memorial Hospital was staked out by television and radio crews trying to interview Kirsty. Fortunately, the ambulance driver didn't stop and, instead, drove around to the rear of the hospital. Two orderlies were waiting with a gurney. Despite my protests, they laid me on it and wheeled me down a corridor to a consulting room where a middle-aged, tired looking doctor and a pretty young nurse started fussing over me.

"You're quite the hero, Mr. Kennelly," the doctor remarked, as he took my blood pressure and the nurse mopped my forehead with a damp cloth. "One-twenty over eighty. You're a fit young man, but that's an extremely nasty scar on your forearm. What happened?"

"It's something I don't care to talk about, Doc. I'm fine. Your time would be better spent attending to those who really need you."

"You might feel okay now, but the shock and trauma of what you've been through will eventually surface," the doctor said as he undid my shirt with bony hands and placed his stethoscope on my chest. "Physically, as I'm sure you know, you're in incredible shape, but you're most certainly going to need counseling."

I looked at the sallow-faced doctor and asked, "Are you going to be my counselor, Doc? You sure look like you could do with some sleep."

"I'm in the twenty-sixth hour of my shift. The hospital is severely short staffed, and the patients just keep on coming." The doctor sighed. "After I finish your medical examination, one of the hospital's senior counselors will see you. Mr. Kennelly, be aware that you may need counseling for up to a year before you fully recover."

"Doc, I was on the frontline in Afghanistan and Iraq for five years. I don't need counseling."

"So that's where you got all the scars on your body? I didn't mention them because you got so annoyed when I asked you about the one on your arm. You must have been involved in some heavy fighting."

I didn't respond. "You tell your counselors to see someone who needs their expertise because I'm getting out of here," I said, swinging my legs off the gurney. "I still have to make a statement to the police."

"Mr. Kennelly, I wouldn't if I were–"

"Yeah, but you're not me, Doc. Thanks for your help, and don't take this the wrong way, but I sure hope I don't see you again anytime soon."

Doctors and nurses scurried along the corridors, orderlies wheeled patients on gurneys into wards and consulting rooms. Post-op patients walked and shuffled along, getting a dose of exercise. The hospital had an unparalleled reputation within the community, and the compassion and skill of its medical staff were highly regarded. In all the activity, no one paid any attention to me. I skirted the waiting room, made my way to the lobby and out the sliding double doors to the portico entrance. In my haste to get out and avoid Officer Enright, I'd forgotten about the media.

"There he is," one of the reporters shouted. Flash bulbs momentarily blinded me. When my eyes cleared, there were three television cameras in my face and questions were coming from all directions. "Were you scared when you were out on the ledge?" "What was going through your mind?" "Have you seen Kirsty?" "How is she?" "Did you know the man who died?"

"Hold on, hold on," I said, but it had no effect.

A pushy female shoved a microphone under my nose. "Were you injured? Why were you in the hospital?"

"I'm fine. They just wanted to give me a routine checkup."

"You were very heroic. Did you fear for your own life when Mr. Evert fell?"

"I wasn't heroic."

"From the time that madman forced the girl out of the window, everything was televised. We know exactly what happened," a chubby reporter with piggy eyes and a knowing smile said.

I felt the heat rush to my cheeks. "If you know so much, you would have seen him trying to get Kirsty back inside. He wasn't a madman. He was a good man looking for help. I feel sorry for him and his family. Why don't you ask the cop who shot him why his trigger finger was so itchy?"

I was wondering how I could get away when a taxi pulled up just past the entrance to the hospital and its two passengers alighted. As it started to pull away, I ran after it and jumped into the front seat next to the burly cabbie who immediately hit the brakes. "I've got another fare to pick up just around the corner. Now get out," he snapped.

"Don't turn the meter on. Just drop me off when you pick up your next fare, and you can pocket this," I said, passing him twenty bucks.

"I can do that, buddy," he said, his scowl turning to a grin.

Chapter 4

AFTER THE CABBIE HAD dumped me, I decided that I needed to clear my head. I was renting an apartment near Pier 39 about three miles away, and I broke out into an easy jog. I ran along Bush Street, turned into Kearny, and then quickened the tempo along Sansome Street. The rapidly thickening fog reduced visibility to about twenty yards, and I found myself running faster and faster. I wanted to feel pain, to hurt, and I wondered whether I was experiencing some type of psychological response to my failure to save Toby Evert. Sixteen minutes later I was home, spent, and drenched in sweat but the endorphins kicked in hard, and my mind was clear. The block of apartments had seen far better times, and the salt air had eroded the paint and was eating away at the mortar. I couldn't complain though. My first-floor studio unit was probably the cheapest in the area. It was close to the main drag where you could buy anything from a loaf of bread to a few milligrams of heroin and everything else in between.

The stench of vomit at the entrance to the ground floor apartment near the bottom of the stairwell overpowered me. I held my breath, jumped over the disgusting yellow mess, and took the stairs two at a time. The dirty cream door to my first-floor apartment was flaking paint, and I hurriedly inserted my key and entered. The khaki carpet was threadbare and moldy, and the air was musty. However, when compared to the smell of what I'd just jumped over, it was like pure oxygen, and I sucked it into my lungs. There was a small living/bedroom which contained a second-hand sofa/fold out bed and a small coffee table. The kitchenette's appliances were comprised of a small refrigerator, a microwave, a kettle and a washer-dryer. The highlight of the apartment, if you could call it that, was a sixteen-inch television with a built-in DVD recorder and player. I found out the agent had taken possession of it from the former tenant in lieu of unpaid rent. The same agent had tried to convince me to enter a twelve-month lease saying that apartments like this were in fierce demand, but I insisted on six months. I didn't care what it looked like so long as it was cheap. It was a place to sleep and eat. I grabbed a bottle of mineral water from the fridge, flicked on the television, and settled down to watch the news. I hadn't remotely considered that I'd be the day's major news item, and clearly, the fog hadn't impeded the cameras.

There I was with my bare feet gripping the ledge like a monkey. I easily worked my way past Kirsty's petite body and then struggled to get around Evert's generous girth. Evert had tried to get Kirsty back to the open window but had frozen. Sweat poured off his bald head and ran down his forehead. Mist and the light drizzle had steamed up his spectacles, and he could no longer see. Lieutenant Rafter, just inside the window, yelled at Evert to drop the knife. Evert, scared but defiant, said that he wasn't going to drop the knife. Kirsty was hysterical and screaming that she was going to die.

I'd spoken softly and soothingly, and the television stations' audio hadn't picked up my words. I guess the helicopters were too noisy. I had said, "Don't worry, Mr. Evert, I'm going to get you safely inside. I'll put my toes on your heels and push. We're going to slowly shuffle off the ledge. It's only three yards. I've got you. You're safe, and you've got Kirsty, so she's safe. Kirsty, take Mr. Evert's glasses off and clean them."

Kirsty screamed that she couldn't, but I knew I had to get her to focus or we might all die.

"Kirsty, Mr. Evert has a daughter about your age. The last thing he's going to do is let you fall, but you'll be safer if he can see."

"What do you know about Georgie?" Evert demanded.

"I know she loves you," I replied.

"Yes, she does." Evert sniffled.

I breathed a little easier when Kirsty reached out and took Evert's glasses and cleaned them on her blouse. His shirt was saturated. I could feel the dampness on my right arm. Lieutenant Rafter was leaning out the window waiting to help Kirsty, but, as we drew closer, she teetered and lost balance. Evert's right arm moved like a bolt of lightning, and he grabbed her shoulder with his fist that was still clenched around the knife. The shot deafened me. I was disoriented and felt spray in my eyes. It took only a split second to refocus on Evert. His shirt was soaked in blood, half his right shoulder was shot away, and he was swaying. I made a desperate grab for him, but he was heavy, and his shirt slipped through my hands. He didn't utter a sound as he went over the edge, and I wondered if the shock had killed him. Lieutenant Rafter dragged Kirsty to safety, but she had lost it completely, and her screams pierced the now deathly silence. There was something wrong that I couldn't put my finger on. I regretted not recording the news and made a note to myself to record the replay later tonight. I flicked to another news channel hoping I might see it again.

I was surprised to see footage of me getting angry with the chubby reporter at the hospital. The newscaster said that I had been incredibly brave and that I was a reluctant young hero. I hated her last two words insofar as they applied to me. There were close-ups of my face, and I cursed my luck. I hoped it wasn't a big enough story to go national. I certainly didn't want it shown in Texas, particularly not in Floydada.

Mercifully the newscaster moved onto the next story about the armed holdup of a downtown jewelry store. I pondered what had driven a family man like Toby Evert to take the law into his own hands. My thoughts were interrupted by the ringing of my phone, a rare occurrence. I let it ring.

It was after seven o'clock when I called Lieutenant Rafter, and I didn't expect him to pick up. He did and immediately whaled into me about leaving Officer Enright in the waiting room of the Jimmy Carter.

"I'm sorry I did that to Vicki," I said, "but I needed a break. I'd had enough of cops for one day."

"Yeah, yeah," he responded, "when are you coming in to make your statement?"

"Can I do it now?"

"I'll be waiting for you," he said.

My statement took nearly two hours, and by the time I got back to my apartment, I was tired and hungry. I made a couple of cheese and ham sandwiches and was just about to sit down when my phone rang. I was completely taken aback. It was Paul Wiese, Summit's senior investment adviser. I'd been with the firm for more than a year, but he had never deigned to introduce himself or speak to me. "Josh, I just want to know how you're holding up? You were incredibly courageous today, and the firm is proud of you."

"I'm all right, Mr. Wiese. I just feel bad about Mr. Evert losing his life."

"Mr. Wiese was my father, Josh. I'm Paul. You have nothing to beat yourself up about. You did everything you could."

"Do you know why Mr. Evert was upset? He said something about bad investments and not being able to get his money back."

"No, I don't. You know what it's like though. We're long-term investors, and we let our clients know that. Because we don't return twenty-five percent in the first two months of their investment, they want to cash out. Show me a firm of investment advisers without dissatisfied clients, and I'll show you the eighth wonder of the world."

"Yeah, I suppose so," I said, but I knew I was being snowed.

"Simon Eisler and I would like to see you first thing in the morning. We think your talent is wasted doing tax returns. Would you like to get involved in the investment side of the business? There will be a nice salary increase plus you'll be entitled to a commission."

"I don't mind doing tax returns."

"Josh, you're tired. You've had a huge day. Why don't you try and get a good night's sleep? I'm sure you'll be thinking more clearly in the morning. Goodnight."

"Yeah, goodnight."

I put my head on my pillow, stared at the ceiling, and saw Toby Evert silently falling through the air. I knew I'd have no problem blocking the image out, but the faces of those two little kids in Afghanistan that had haunted me for years were something else.

Chapter 5

WHEN I AWOKE, I watched the late-night news that I'd recorded. I was unable to find what I was looking for in the footage. After I had watched it four times, I gave up. The fact was that I didn't know what I was looking for. I just had a gut feeling that something was wrong.

I turned the television on to KGO-TV. The presenter was speculating about the string of SFPD fatal, officer-involved shootings, including that of Tobias Evert. I hadn't realized it, but the SFPD had been the subject of investigations by the Justice Department and the State's District Attorney. A spokesman for the SFPD said he couldn't comment on the circumstances surrounding Tobias Evert's death and that the investigation was ongoing.

I flicked to another channel. The presenter was pondering what might have driven Toby Evert to take such drastic action and whether it was random or specifically related to Summit Investments. She talked about what a tragedy it was for Evert's wife and daughter. A family pic, obviously quite a few years old flashed across the screen. Evert's wife was Indian, petite and very attractive. The red dot in the middle of her forehead told me that she was Hindu and probably very religious. Modern Hindu women wore bindis as fashion accessories, but I knew that wouldn't be the case with Evert's wife. Their daughter was fair-haired and gangly with large horn-rimmed glasses and pigtails. Fortunately, the presenter hadn't mentioned me, and I hoped my fifteen minutes of fame was over.

I turned the radio on to KCBS and listened to some fierce exchanges between the talkback jock and his callers. Two policemen had been suspended pending a full investigation, the shooter, who for some reason couldn't be named, and Lieutenant Rafter. There was no debate about the shooter, but listeners were incensed about Rafter. He'd been suspended for letting me go out on the ledge. I cursed. Anything that kept my name in the limelight could serve no good.

I showered, had a bowl of cereal and washed it down with orange juice. I felt refreshed and bounded down the stairwell. The vomit had congealed. I leaped across it, turned the door handle, and shoved the door open in one motion.

As the door closed, I saw half a dozen reporters converging on me with their cameras and recording devices. "There he is," one shouted. "Did Mr. Evert tell you why he did it before he fell?"

"Do you think the police Lieutenant should've been suspended?" an aggressive young woman asked, almost pushing her microphone into my mouth.

Another demanded to know whether I thought the shooter should be charged with manslaughter or murder. They were like piranhas. I pulled the door open, raced up the stairs, and locked myself in my apartment. The last thing I needed was more exposure.

I called Paul Wiese to tell him that I was trapped and wouldn't be able to make the meeting. I heard a voice in the background say, "He's a bloody hero. What's wrong with him? The media want to laud him. Tell him to get out there and talk to them."

"Did you hear that, Josh?"

"What?" I said.

"I'm with Simon. We think you should talk to them. It's not like you did anything wrong. The phones have been going crazy with clients wanting to praise and congratulate you. You're a hero. It'll be good PR for the firm if you speak to the media. They're not going to give up until you do. Just get it over with."

"I'm nervous, and I like my privacy," I said, having never suffered from nerves. "I don't want to come across as a doofus and embarrass myself or the firm."

"For Chrissakes," Paul said, "do it and then get in here. We've got big plans for you. You're gonna be very pleased. Call us when you're on your way."

"I can't."

"Why?"

"I don't have a cell phone."

I heard Eisler say, "Oh, fuck I don't believe it. What century's this kid living in?"

"I'm no kid. I'll see you in half an hour," I said and hung up.

There was a small, smoked glass window in the bathroom with one of those wind out mechanisms. I grabbed a chair to stand on and wound it as far as it would go. If I could get my head through the gap, I knew I could pull my body through. It was a tight squeeze, but after a few minutes shimmying, I pushed the fly wire screen out and dropped to the parking lot at the rear of the apartments. I climbed over the fence at the rear into an adjoining apartment block and ran out onto Battery Street. There was no sign of the media.

I jumped on a cable car to Union Square and did some quick shopping at Macy's. One of the shop assistants in menswear said, "Oh, you're the guy who was on the ledge. You were so brave." I thanked her, selected a navy-blue hoodie from the rack and tried it on. I asked her to cut the labels off and wore it with the hood up when I walked out onto O'Farrell Street

It was nearly 10 A.M. when I got to the office. I smiled at the temporary receptionist who had the name tag Mandy pinned on her blouse. She returned my smile and said, "Oh, it's you," and handed me at least fifty messages, which was more than I'd received in the prior twelve months. "I watched you on television, Mr. Kennelly. You were fantastic."

Managers and employees, some who I'd never met before, went out of their way to shake my hand. It was a good ten minutes before I reached my cubicle, and even then, the back slapping continued. Libby, the dorky new girl who occupied the cubicle next to mine, even asked if I'd like a cup of coffee. I'd been with Summit for more than a year, and this was a first. I flicked through my messages and didn't recognize any of the callers.

As I picked up the phone, Simon Eisler's voice came over the intercom. "Josh, I'm with Paul. Come down to my office." This was another first. Mr. Eisler had never spoken to me. I made my way down to the executive suite. Barbara Sumner was Eisler's PA. She was in her mid-twenties and quite attractive, but she had a hard, almost chiseled face. She gave me a mechanical smile and flicked her long brunette hair when she stood up. "Follow me," she said, and my eyes involuntarily dropped to her shapely butt and slender legs.

Eisler's corner office took my breath away. It overlooked California Street and was the largest and most luxurious office I'd ever been in. A large walnut desk and leather chairs were on the south side of the room, and there was a coffee table with matching chairs adjacent to it. On the north side of the room, was a boardroom table. I could see a well-stocked bar behind the partially open doors, built into the teak wall paneling. What looked like expensive paintings adorned the walls. A built-in bookshelf took the complete wall next to the boardroom table, and it was filled with prospectuses, financial journals and investment reports facing out for easy access. Simon Eisler and Paul Wiese were sitting at the boardroom table with a number of documents in front of them.

Eisler got up and shook my hand vigorously while putting his left arm around my shoulders like we were long lost buddies. He was about forty, tall and lean with strong hands. "Josh, it's a pleasure to meet you. Where have you been hiding the past few years? You're a brave young man."

"It was nothing, Mr. Eisler," I said.

"Nothing? What you did was beyond courageous. The phones have been going mad with clients wanting to congratulate you. I bet your parents are proud of you. Oh, and call me Simon. Can I get you a drink? Mineral water, orange juice, champagne?" He laughed.

"Nothing, thanks," I replied. "My parents passed away years ago." The truth was I didn't know who my birth parents were. My adoptive mother had passed away when I was thirteen and my adoptive father two years later. I don't know whether they would've been proud. They were poor, sullen people who'd kept to themselves and they may well have been upset with the publicity their adopted son had foisted upon them.

"You know, Josh," Eisler said, nodding toward Wiese. "We've been discussing your future. Grab a chair, and you can let us know what you think of our plans."

Eisler was staring at me intently.

Chapter 6

PAUL WIESE PICKED UP one of the brochures and handed it to me. I looked at the glossy pictures of huge ships, container depots, and shipping containers and wondered where this was going. "This is the greatest investment of the twenty-first century," Wiese said, "the humble shipping container."

"Yeah, you're right, Paul, but you're getting ahead of yourself," Eisler said. "I want to talk about Josh's future. Josh, what you did yesterday has made you and the firm the talk of the town, and we want to capital–"

"Simon," Barbara's voice came over the intercom, "it's–"

"For Chrissake, Barbara. I told you no interruptions," Eisler said, his mouth contorted and his blue eyes cold.

"It's Mr. Lowy. He said if I don't put him through he's going to come in, close his account and withdraw his funds. I thought you'd want to talk to him."

"Jesus! Yeah, put him through. Hello, Sol. How may I help you?" Eisler said.

I couldn't hear what Mr. Lowy was saying, but it soon became apparent.

"No, Sol, the firm is profitable, highly cashed up and you should know better than anyone that we're delivering for our clients. What was your return last year? Twenty, twenty-five percent? Sadly, Mr. Evert was deranged, mentally unbalanced, and decided to take it out on us. I wish we could have saved him."

I glanced at Paul Wiese and thought I saw him wink. He looked at me and brushed his wrist across his eyes as if he was wiping something from them. Perhaps I was wrong.

"Yes, yes, he's sitting in my office. Yes, you're not wrong. He's a fine young man, and if it weren't for him, there would have been two lives lost yesterday. I'm going to be moving him into the investment side of the business as one of Paul's assistants."

Eisler was smiling and nodding. "If you'd like him to work on your account that can be arranged. Yes, Josh Kennelly, and I can organize that. It's not every day that you get to have lunch with a full-blown hero, is it?"

Eisler ran a hand through his thick silver hair. "Sol, if you're worried about your money, come in and see me. I'll have a check waiting for you. The container fleet had close to a hundred percent utilization this quarter, so I expect a significant income distribution. You'll miss out on that, but if you're losing sleep, I'd rather give your money back to you."

Eisler laughed. "Well, that's a turnaround, Sol. No, I'm sorry we can't help you in the short term. The demand for containers is so great that we can't supply them. We're knocking back new investors every day. Yeah, yeah, I know you're not a new investor. Two million? Sol, the only way I can help you increase your investment is by talking another investor into selling, and I couldn't do that. It wouldn't be ethical. You'd get upset if I did it to you. Yeah, you know we'll give you preference over new investors. We always do. Sure, we'll talk soon."

"Is Sol okay?" Wiese asked.

"He's fine, Paul. He wants more containers. Josh, some of our clients have understandably been a little nervous about what happened yesterday. On the plus side, they love what you did.

Half of them want to take you out to dinner, and the other half want you to marry their daughters."

Eisler stared intently at me again. "We've got the same color eyes, and you may not believe it, Josh, but twenty years ago my hair was as blonde as yours." Eisler laughed.

"You were happy to pay Mr. Lowy out. Why didn't you pay Mr. Evert?" I asked.

"We should have. Ocean Cargo Containers provide an undertaking to buy back the containers anytime within the first three years, but the rules provide that the investor must give them twenty-one days' notice. Unfortunately, Mr. Evert spoke to one of our junior investment advisers who didn't know we could bend the rules. If he'd spoken to Paul or me, he'd still be with us."

"But he came in to see you yesterday?" I persisted.

"I was very busy yesterday afternoon. Mr. Evert hadn't made an appointment. The first I knew about him wanting to see me was when he dragged Kirsty out onto the ledge." Eisler said, looking at his watch. "Josh, I'm running short of time. You're too talented to be wasting your time on tax returns. I want you to join Paul's team. Plus, I want you to help promote the firm."

"Yeah." Wiese said, "you're the flavor of the month. We'd like to feature you in some television commercials and web content."

The last thing I wanted was more exposure, but at least I now knew why they were so keen to court me. I had experience in the promotions area. When I'd started to develop a reputation in Iraq and Afghanistan, the army brass told me they wanted to use me in recruitment advertisements. I point blank refused. I didn't want the parents of sons and daughters holding me responsible for their children's deaths. I'd joined the army on the recommendation of the only person I had ever loved so that I could get an education. "I'd be too nervous to get the words out on a television advertisement," I said, "and besides, as I told you, Mr. Wiese, I'm happy doing tax returns."

Eisler frowned. "You need to think this through, Josh. We haven't talked money, but I'm prepared to double your salary and pay you a commission. You'll be able to get out of that shithole you're living in and rent something half decent."

They hadn't known who I was before yesterday. Now they knew my living arrangements. "I don't understand," I said. "Why do you want to advertise? You've got a client with two million dollars looking for shipping containers, and you can't supply them. What's the point in advertising?"

"You've got a lot to learn, Josh. We could've supplied Sol Lowy without any problems, but he's not going anywhere with his cash. He's even concerned that we're supplying others rather than him." Eisler laughed. "If I'd said we could supply immediately, Sol would've put the phone down and worried that there was a surplus of containers that might lead to lower hire rates. Now he's sweating about missing out. Our manufacturers in Shanghai are running their plants twenty-four seven."

"I don't understand," I said. "I thought that world shipping collapsed after the global financial crisis, and it hasn't recovered. How can you get returns of more than twenty percent?"

"It's far more complicated than that," Wiese said. "There are tax concessions, exchange rates, hedging and a variety of other factors that need to be considered in deriving the overall return."

I was being snowed again. I tried to read the Wall Street Journal at least once a week, and I knew the Baltic Dry Index, which measured the price of moving major raw materials by sea, was still falling. "How does it work?" I asked.

"We initially act as a buying agent for our clients. We buy the containers from Ocean Cargo Containers but the ownership vests in our clients. Each container has its own serial number, so no matter what happens our clients have ownership. The clients then rent the containers to a fund that we created and manage. We take a small fixed fee and a share of the income. The fund's made up of a pool of our clients' containers, and while some mightn't be hired in a quarter, their owners still share in the pool's income. Now, here's the beauty of the investment. Ocean Cargo Containers guarantee to buy the containers back after three years for their initial purchase price."

I didn't know much about investing, but this scheme had a real smell to it. I knew that shipping containers took a real battering, so how could the supplier agree to buy them back for their initial purchase price? "Can I have a few days to think about it?" I asked.

"Don't take too long," Eisler said, "popularity is a rapidly diminishing investment. You should be a seller while yours is at its peak."

I thanked them and left Eisler's office. Clearly, they'd expected me to fall over myself saying yes and were not impressed. The increase in salary was certainly attractive, but the risk of being exposed was far too great for me to say yes.

As I walked past Barbara Sumner's desk, she said, "Josh, I have something for you," and handed me two boxes.

I must have looked surprised because with a touch of sarcasm she added, "They contain an iPhone and a laptop. Do you want me to show you how to use them?"

"Thanks, but I'll be okay," I said. I was more than competent. I hadn't had a cell phone or laptop because I'd wanted to remove as many sources of contact as I could.

Chapter 7

THE REST OF THE day was a blur. I'd never returned or received so many phone calls. Most were from clients I'd never spoken to or met. It was more than a little embarrassing talking to people I didn't know who were heaping praise on me. A few of them, after congratulating me, asked me how the firm was traveling, and did they have anything to worry about. I had to say no, but felt compromised. Didn't these people understand that the firm had no liability or responsibility other than hiring their containers out? Protection of their capital was in their ownership of the containers and the undertaking by Ocean Cargo Containers to buy them back. If they didn't know that, I guessed they couldn't have checked the company out. I wondered whether it was a U.S. registered company or if it were incorporated in China or another country. Who were the directors and shareholders and what was its capital? How financially capable was it of meeting its undertakings? As I pondered these questions, I started to feel silly. Of course, Simon Eisler and Paul Wiese would've satisfied themselves as to Ocean Cargo Containers' viability before recommending the container investments to the firm's clients. There were also several calls from reporters and journalists. I did not return them.

Later in the afternoon our receptionist buzzed and said that two detectives from SFPD were in reception and wanted to talk to me. I wondered why. "Is there an interview room free, Mandy?"

"Yes. Number four is free for the rest of the day."

"Good. Show them to it. I'll be there in a few minutes."

When I entered the room, the two detectives were standing. "Matt Lanza," said a heavy-jowled, swarthy man, extending his hand, "and my partner Luke Selwood." He wasn't a local, and, while I'd never been to Chicago, I'd watched enough television to recognize the chipped accent.

"What's this about?" I asked.

"We're got a few routine questions for you. It's just procedural, nothing to worry about." Lanza smiled.

"You got a card?"

"Sure," Lanza said, handing me his card.

I hadn't wanted to rile them by asking for identification, but I did want to satisfy myself they were with the SFPD. The card told me Lanza was a senior detective based at 1251 3rd Street and that was enough for me. "How can I help you, Detective?"

"What happened immediately before you went out onto the ledge?"

"Mr. Evert was on the ledge holding Kirsty. It was starting to rain. There were helicopters above them, and your SWAT team had taken over California Street."

"We know that. We've watched the video. What we want to know is what you said and did before you went out the window?"

"Oh, I kicked my shoes and socks off and out I went. That's it."

"Didn't you ask Lieutenant Rafter if you could go out on the ledge, and didn't he say yes?" Lanza frowned and leaned across the table, cracking his knuckles.

I didn't know what they were looking for, but it was clear that they had Lieutenant Rafter in their sights. "I don't remember. It all happened so fast."

The younger, wiry Selwood smirked and said, "Wasn't Lieutenant Rafter at the window and isn't the opening only big enough for one person. How did you get past him?"

"Good question," I said, putting my hands to my forehead. "I can't swear to it, but I guess I shoved him out of the way. Did you ask Officer Enright?"

"She's under investigation too," Lanza said.

"What's this really about? I've already made a statement."

"Yeah, we've read it," Lanza said. "There's nothing in it about you pushing Lieutenant Rafter out of the way. Strange, isn't it?"

"No. I made my statement that evening in the aftermath of the moment. It covered everything that I thought was important. I'd be happy to change it if that's what you want."

"You shoved him out of the way." Selwood smirked. "I reckon he outweighs you by sixty pounds, and you're hardly Arnold Schwarzenegger, are you? Did he ask you to go out onto that ledge?"

"No. Look, what is this? Why didn't you tell me upfront you were investigating Lieutenant Rafter and Officer Enright? It sounds to me like you're trying to stitch them up. You're looking at the wrong people. You should be looking at the shooter."

Lanza and Selwood, no longer smiling, exchanged glances. I suspected that they wanted to accuse me of telling lies and being a wiseass.

"We're not trying to stitch anyone up," Lanza said. "We're just trying to get to the truth."

I didn't respond, but there was something about these two cops that made me uncomfortable. Why were they after Lieutenant Rafter rather than the shooter?

"Well," Selwood said.

"Well, what?" I replied.

"You have no comment?"

"You didn't ask me a question."

"It's gonna be like that, is it?" Lanza said. "You gotta lot of chutzpah for a baby-faced kid."

Again, I didn't respond, and the room lapsed into an uncomfortable, tense silence. I knew what they were doing. First to speak loses. I'd been in this position plenty of times and had to fight to stop myself from smiling. Instead, I closed my eyes as if I were snoozing.

Selwood was first to break and was nearly shouting when he asked, "Did you hear Lieutenant Rafter tell the SWAT team to fire?"

"No, because he didn't!"

"You were out on the ledge. The helicopters were above you, the wind was howling, and the rain was coming down. You may not have heard him," Lanza chimed in.

"He never stopped talking to Mr. Evert and Kirsty. Never! That's why I know he never gave the order to shoot. Why are you asking me? You had walkie talkies, cell phones, and laptops. I'm sure there's a record of every word spoken."

"There's not," Lanza said. "Unfortunately, the information was corrupted."

"Corrupted?" I grinned. "Interesting choice of words."

"What are you implying, smartass?" Selwood said, getting out of his chair and standing directly in front of me. His face was contorted, and he was shaking.

"Sit down, Len," Lanza ordered.

"Yeah, sit down, Len." I added, "Losing your temper can be bad for your blood pressure."

If looks could kill, I'd be dead.

"Could Officer Enright have given the order to fire?" Lanza asked.

"Of course," I replied, "and so could the Pope, Queen Elizabeth, and the Dalai Lama. Why are you two so anxious to pin the shooting on Rafter and Enright? Here's what happened. A trigger-happy SWAT sniper got it into his mind to release a round that killed Evert and could've quite easily killed his hostage. It was dangerous, uncalled for, and he's the guy who you should be questioning. If the DA's doing his job properly, he'll charge him with manslaughter."

"That's not right," Selwood replied. "The girl was safe. Lieutenant Rafter had both his hands wrapped firmly around her arm. There was no possibility of her falling. Officer Pen–"

Lanza interrupted, glaring at Selwood. "We're going over old ground," he said. Obviously, he didn't want the shooter's name revealed. It didn't make any difference to me. What was I going to do? More importantly, I now realized what I'd missed on the video. The point of the knife was vertical in Evert's hand. No matter what angle anyone was looking from, it was apparent that Kirsty was in no danger. The shooter would've seen Kirsty slip, and Evert raise his arm, the one holding the knife to steady her, and Rafter wrap his hands around Kirsty's arm. The shooter had fired the split-second Rafter was dragging Kirsty through the window, but why?

"So, if she were safe, Detective, why did the shooter fire?"

"It's so easy for you," Lanza said. "You've probably never faced a moment's danger in your sheltered, cushy life, but when you do, who do you call first? The cops who you love to bag, that's who. The officer thought that Evert was going to use the knife and acted. Who's to say he wasn't going to use it?"

"Me. He'd helped Kirsty safely traverse three to four yards across the ledge. The knife was never at an angle that suggested he was going to use it, and Kirsty was directly in front of the open window."

"That's what you're going to tell the Coroner?"

"Or the court if the shooter's charged before the inquest," I said, wondering what his name was. I had the first three letters, and SFPD SWAT couldn't have too many officers with a surname starting Pen. "Don't worry, I'm going to tell the whole truth and nothing but the truth, just like they do in the movies."

Lanza pushed himself back from the table and got up still cracking the knuckles of his meaty hands. "You're batting way out of your league, kid. If you know what's good for you, you'll be careful."

"Is that right? I heard the SFPD's being investigated by the Justice Department and the State's District Attorney over fatal officer-involved shootings. Tell me, Detective Lanza, why didn't you make notes or record this interrogation?"

"Interrogation?" Lanza laughed, as he opened the door. "This wasn't an interrogation, it was a friendly meeting. If we ever haul you into 3rd Street, you'll get to find out what an interrogation is then."

"That sounds like a threat to me," I said.

"You've got a vivid imagination," Lanza replied. "We'll see you around."

After they'd left, I sat at the coffee table pondering what they had said. They didn't like Rafter and Enright and were doing everything they could to protect the shooter. The video looped around in my head, and there was no justification for the shooter firing. If it weren't so stupid, I'd say it was murder, but what was the motive and how could it have been premeditated? No, it was just a trigger-happy cop who made a fatal mistake.

Chapter 8

THE NEXT FEW DAYS returned to almost normal. Calls from clients wanting to congratulate me dried up. I was no longer the news of the day, and the media stopped calling. I hadn't received any calls from Floydada, so I presumed the story hadn't been telecast in Texas. That was a relief. Eisler and Wiese continued to pressure me for an answer to their offer, and I continued to stall. I could've just said no, but I didn't want to insult them by appearing not to have given their offer careful consideration.

There was no way that I was going to appear in television and internet commercials. I'd been lucky that no one had recognized me on the news and I wasn't going to push my luck. Besides, I didn't understand enough about the business or its investment products to vouch for or recommend them. I let Eisler and Wiese know of my misgivings. Despite this, they arranged for an advertising agency's production crew to come in and shoot some footage of me. Late on Thursday afternoon I received a phone call from the advertising agency's production coordinator, Monica Wood, who told me what I should wear. I wasn't worried. I'd handle it in the same way I had when the army's cameras focused on me. I was looking forward to getting it over with, putting my feet up and relaxing on the weekend.

When I arrived at the office on Friday morning, I was wearing jeans, suede loafers, a casual shirt, and my smartest jacket. I was carrying another three casual shirts. Ten minutes later, I went out to reception to meet Monica Wood. She was small, but her parts were big, and like her, loud — big red hair, big red lips and a matching mouth, big boobs and really high heels. She was wearing a charcoal gray pants suit and a tight black top.

"I'm Monica." she said. "We're going to start shooting with the bridge and the bay as the background. Then we'll move onto the second shoot at Sausalito. Let's go. We've got no time to waste." We took an elevator to the parking garage, and she led me to a small red BMW. As we exited, she handed me two scripts and said, "read these." Two white vans waiting at the front of the building followed us through the city streets.

Looking for investment advice you can trust?

Then look no further than my colleagues and me at Summit Investments.

We've built our reputation on trust.

Don't lose sleep at night. Trust us.

Pick up the phone and call an adviser right now. Trust us? Sure can.

I didn't read the second script because I knew we wouldn't be making it to Sausalito. I wasn't an expert on the law relating to investment advice, but it seemed to me that I was claiming to be an investment adviser. I wasn't, and I suspected when I uttered the words in the script, I'd be breaking the law.

"Think you can handle it?" Monica asked.

"I-I d-don't know," I replied. "I-I'm very ner-ner-nervous."

"Christ, I wasn't told you're a bloody stutterer," she said. "It's only five lines. You'll just have to concentrate and do exactly what I tell you. You won't have to think of anything. I'll tell you when to look sincere, when to smile, and when to frown. You'll be fine."

I could tell this woman was a high achiever, used to handing out orders and being obeyed. I felt sorry for her. She was going to be disappointed. Our little convoy stopped on the city side of the bridge, and the camera crews got set up. A makeup artist worked her magic on my face while Monica chose a shirt for me.

"You're not into fashion are you?" she said. "We should've stopped and bought you something decent. It's too late now, but we might find something in Sausalito for the second shoot."

"Ye-yeah," I replied.

It was 11:00 a.m. when the shoot got underway, and I said, "Loo-Loo-Looking for invest-investment ad-advice you ca-can tru-trust?"

"No," Monica shouted, "get a hold of yourself and for Chrissake stop the stuttering. You're meant to look sincere, not miserable. Get a grip, I told you to look at the camera on the left, and you stared at the one on the right."

"I-I-I'm real-really ner-nervous."

"I can tell that. Just concentrate."

"O-Okay."

By 3:00 p.m., Monica was beside herself with anger. I smiled when I heard her say to the makeup artist, "He may be good looking and courageous, but he's as dumb as dog shit."

Ten minutes later she yelled, "That's it. Pack the gear up. We're finished." She had no usable footage, and my stutter had deteriorated

"Wha-what ab-about Sau-Saus-Sausalito?" I asked.

"Are you kidding me?" she said. "Get in the car and don't say anything. I don't want to hear another wor-wor-word out of you."

Monica was fuming on the drive back to the city, and the

tension was palpable. As she pulled up and I opened the door, a strange look came over her face, as if she'd just remembered something. "You prick. You lowdown prick," she said. "I watched you answer the media's questions at the Jimmy Carter Memorial. There wasn't so much as an umm let alone a stutter. You faked it today. Why?"

I kicked myself. I'd completely overlooked the exchange I'd had with the media at the hospital. "Th-that was spon-spon-spontaneous," I said, "I-I did-didn't have ti-time to get ner-nervous."

She glared at me, and I could see her mind working overtime. "Fa-Far-fuck off you-you ass-ass-asshole," she said, as she burnt rubber down California Street.

Paul Wiese was waiting for me in the lobby. His spectacles sat on the end of his nose, and his comb-over flopped limply in the middle of his forehead rather than covering his balding temple. He put his thumbs into his vest pockets and pulled himself up to his full five foot six inches. "What are you playing at, Josh? You cost us a lot of money today. Simon's seething. Monica told him you sabotaged the shoot. Is that true?"

I didn't need this shit or these pricks, but I bit my tongue knowing I still had to pay the rent. "I told you I suffered from nerves and you ignored me. I didn't sabotage anything, it just happened."

Wiese compressed his lips into a thin smirk. "Yeah, yeah. I bet," he said. "You don't have to worry about the job offer, it's off the table, and, if Simon doesn't calm down over the weekend, you won't have a job on Monday."

With his black vest and white shirt, he reminded me of a

rotund little penguin, and I had to stop myself from laughing. "I'm sorry, Mr. Wiese," I said.

This time he didn't tell me to call him Paul. As he waddled off down the corridor, the receptionist gave me a sympathetic smile. I was glad it was nearly quittin' time.

Chapter 9

I TIDIED MY LITTLE cubicle and looked around wondering whether I'd still have a job on Monday. I had planned to do nothing over the weekend, but now I'd be on the net looking for jobs. There was no point beating myself up though. I'd done what I had to do.

I stepped off the elevator and made my way across the foyer at a brisk pace, through the large revolving door and onto the street. I'd only walked a few steps when I felt a tugging on my sleeve and turned to see a sad, willowy, young woman.

"Can I talk to you, Mr. Kennelly? I'm Tobias Evert's daughter, Georgie."

My mind raced back to the family photo, and I thought what an incredible metamorphosis. She had golden skin, big brown eyes, a little button nose and generous pink lips. "I'm sorry about your father," I said.

"You were very brave. Thank you for risking your life to save him. Please, I have to talk to you."

"That's fine. Would you like to go to a bar or would you prefer a coffee shop?"

"I don't drink," she replied, "but I'm happy with either. I could have mineral water."

"I know a great coffee shop just around the corner on Montgomery," I said. "I'm sure it'll be quieter than a bar."

The Workshop Café was a bit techie and a haven for those

with laptops and tablets. I liked it because it was warm and cozy. The waiters were friendly. The coffee was great. The hot chocolate was to die for. It was clean, and I could hear myself think. After we were seated and had ordered hot chocolates, Georgie took off her pale, pink leather jacket and put it on the adjoining seat. She was wearing a figure-hugging black skirt and a crisp white blouse. "Thank you for seeing me, Mr. Kennelly."

"No one's ever called me Mr. Kennelly before. I'm Josh." I smiled, extending my hand.

"Mr—Josh, did you know about my father's investments?"

"No, I'm not involved in that side of the business. I help out with the tax returns."

Georgie looked disappointed. "Oh, you're an accountant?"

"I'm a nothing," I replied. "I know a little about taxation, and I prepare clients' tax returns, but my work is always reviewed and signed off by a senior accountant."

"Oh," she said. "I'm sorry I'm wasting your time."

Our hot chocolates arrived, and I took a sip. The taste was rich, indulgent and almost decadent.

"Georgie, two heads are better than one. I sense you want to get something off your chest, and I promise, anything you tell me will go no further."

She sighed. "You're right. Dad was very conservative, but before the global financial crisis, his stockbrokers talked him into margining his account. He had what he thought was a blue-chip portfolio. Merrill Lynch, Freddie Mac, Bear Stearns, Lehman's, IBM and other major companies. He'd been a successful investor over the years, but I recall him saying that he'd lost fifteen years' profits and dividends in just six months. He never blamed his stockbrokers who, by the way, went broke. He said that it was all his fault and that he'd been stupid and greedy."

"The GFC wiped out some of the world's best investors."

"Yes, dad said the same thing. He lost millions but he wasn't wiped out, and we were left with the house in Sausalito and some cash. I don't know how much. He was convinced the market would eventually turn and was determined to get back what he'd lost."

"Sorry," I interrupted, "but how did Summit get involved?"

"I was coming to that. Dad was on a flight to LA, and Simon Eisler was sitting next to him. Dad said it was the luckiest day of his life and that Eisler was a financial genius. He put all of his money with Summit and got involved in buying blue chip shares and selling options over them. Dad did very well and was making more than twenty percent per annum consistently."

I caught our waiter's eye and ordered another two hot chocolates. "Would you like anything to eat, Georgie?"

"No thanks, but don't let me stop you," she replied.

I wasn't going to eat in front of her. "I'm fine. Your father was doing well. What was the problem?"

"Well, dad got worried about the size of his portfolio six months ago and asked Simon Eisler to sell a million dollars of his investments. Eisler fobbed him off and then wouldn't take his calls. Dad called me and was going up the wall. Even when the GFC was at its worst, he never got that stressed."

"Hang on, are you saying that Summit was acting as an agent or power of attorney for your father? Why did he call rather than discuss it with you at home?"

"I don't live at home. I'm a web designer in New York. I don't know what dad's legal relationship with Summit was. However, he called me about three months ago, more stressed than ever. He was almost incoherent and said something about all his money being invested in shipping containers. Then, in the week be-before he was kill-killed—"

Instinctively I reached out and took Georgie's hand. It was cold, and she was trembling. Her pupils were dilated, and I knew she was fighting back the tears. "Hey, it's all right. Would you like to take a minute to powder your nose?"

"I'm sorry. I'm okay now. It's still hard to believe he's gone. Last week he told me that he was seriously ill. That he'd lost more than three million dollars and the house as well. He was going to Summit to see Eisler, and he wasn't leaving until he had a check."

I was still holding Georgie's hand and patted it as a prelude to withdrawing it, but she held on even tighter.

"The day after dad was shot, mom got a letter of foreclosure from the bank claiming that they were behind on their mortgage payments and demanding nearly one and a quarter million dollars. I'm not even sure the house is worth that," Georgie said, wiping away a tear.

"Does your mom remember signing the mortgage documents?"

"No, but she would've signed anything dad put in front of her. Can you help?" she asked, her big brown eyes engulfing me.

Her impact had been enormous. She had an honesty and innocence that was so appealing. I had never felt like this about a girl on a first meeting before, so I responded, "Yes," without having any idea what I could do.

As if reading my thoughts, she asked, "What do you have in mind?"

"Nothing yet," I said truthfully, "but trust me, I'll think of something. Your father's money can't just have disappeared into thin air."

"I've kept you long enough," she said, looking at her watch. "It's nearly nine o'clock, and I promised mom I wouldn't be late."

Before we left the café, we exchanged phone numbers. As we walked out onto Montgomery, we were hit by a cold gust of wind. I took my jacket off and despite Georgie's protests, wrapped it around her shoulders. I put my arm around her. "Let's find you a taxi," I said.

We walked to California Street, and I hailed a cab that pulled up next to us. Georgie turned around and smiled for the first time since I'd met her. I was nearly thirty, but no smile had ever hit me so hard. "Thanks, Josh, I'll call you," she said, kissing me on the cheek before disappearing into the back seat of the taxi.

I stood on the street shivering and wondered what I was going to do. For the first time, I was concerned about being fired on Monday, knowing that, if that occurred, there'd be nothing I could do to help Georgie.

Chapter 10

IT TOOK ME FORTY minutes to walk home, and as I approached my apartment, I saw that the security light that had been working the night before had failed. Then I saw the embers of a cigarette. The smoker and two of his friends were blocking the entrance, and I said, "Excuse me. Can I get through please?"

They were wearing dark full-length coats, and the heavyset smoker was wearing a hat like Cagney, Edward G, and Bogart used to wear in the thirties. "Josh, you're quite the hero, aren't you?" he said.

"Do I know you?" I asked, trying to get a look at the man's face. I couldn't see his hair, but he had red, bushy eyebrows and a hard, unshaven face.

"No, we've never met," he said, "but everyone knows you. You're the big man, aren't you?"

As he was talking, the two other men sidled past me, and I sensed that they were positioning themselves to block me if I ran, or perhaps they were just getting ready to give me a beating.

"What is this? You obviously have a gripe with me. What have I done? If I can fix it, I will."

The smoker laughed and said to his buddies, "Josh, wants to know what he's done to upset us. Why don't you tell him, Joe?"

I turned to look at the man, and the smoker was immediately behind me. It didn't matter which way I faced, one of them was always behind me. I felt my heart beat starting to slow, and a calmness consumed me. I'd felt it many times before.

"Where are you from, Josh?" Joe asked.

"Floydada, Texas."

"Ah, I thought I detected a trace of Texas in that accent. Why would a good old Texas boy come to our fine city and tip a bucket over those who are protecting us?" Joe said, lobbing a glob of spit an inch in front of my shoes.

"You're the police?"

"No, we're not," the smoker said, "but we do support San Francisco's finest and don't like it when they're attacked, particularly by a no good, out-of-stater."

"I haven't said anything derogatory about the police."

"Now that's a lie! A downright, filthy lie. You're not the only hero in town, you know. Don't you think that was a mighty fine piece of shooting that took that lunatic out?" The man next to Joe said.

"Ah, so that's what this is about," I said. "What's your name?"

"He's Joe Two," the smoker said, "and, before you ask, I'm Joe Three."

"You don't get any marks for originality," I said.

"We were told you were a wiseass. I'd be careful if I were you. We're not like the police. We don't have to follow any rules," the smoker said.

I could feel them pressing in on me and didn't need to be a Philadelphia Lawyer to know what they had planned.

"You still haven't told me what you want."

"We heard that you think the police shooter should be charged with manslaughter, and you're going to testify that way," Joe said.

"No, no, that's not true," I said.

"You've seen the light," the smoker smirked, pushing his face up against mine. "You're too late. It's not going to help you now."

"Yeah, on reflection, I think he should be charged with murder. There was no need to fire. He killed a harmless family man."

"You worthless piece of shit," the smoker growled. "You're not gonna recognize your pretty face in the morning."

I wasn't worried, but I was looking for a way not to fight when a car pulled up with its lights on high beam momentarily blinding the three thugs. At that moment, I was running, knowing that there was no way they were going to catch me. I reached the corner of the building when a bullet ricocheted off it no more than ten feet from me. I couldn't hear them chasing me, but the last thing I'd expected was to be shot at, and I shifted up to top gear and broke into a full sprint. I knew where I was headed. The Pub at Ghirardelli Square on Beach Street stayed open until after midnight, and I'd be safe there.

I took a few minutes to regain my breath and wipe the sweat from my face before entering The Pub. It wasn't crowded, and I sat down on a stool at the bar and ordered a mineral water. I didn't know who those guys were, but I suspected cops. They knew everything that I had told Lanza and Selwood. Yet again, would cops open fire on a civilian on the street? I answered my own question. The shot hadn't even been close. It was a warning shot. They were trying to scare me.

Two hours later when I got back to my apartment, there was no sign of the thugs. I crept gingerly up the stairs on full alert. They had left but not without leaving a message. Nailed to my door was the bloody carcass of a headless chicken, its symbolism evident. No doubt my neighbors and those using the stairs had seen it, but they wouldn't have reported it because it was barely outside what passed for normal in this area. I took it down, put it in a plastic bag and threw it in one of the large trash bins. Ten minutes of solid scrubbing got rid of the gizzards and most of the blood on the door.

Chapter 11

I AWOKE ON SATURDAY morning and pondered the events of the previous night. I was certain the three thugs were cops and that they'd been sent to warn me off truthfully testifying.

I wanted to call Georgie but resisted the temptation. I hardly knew her and couldn't share what had happened to me when I got home. She had made a huge impression, was on my mind, and I foolishly hoped she might call. I also thought about Lanza and Selwood, Toby Evert, the shipping containers and Summit, and tried to fathom what was going on, but I was way out of my depth. However, I was a deadly accurate judge of character, and I didn't like Eisler or Wiese. There was something about them that I couldn't quite put my finger on. If I were looking to invest my little nest egg, they'd be the last two from whom I'd take advice.

I'd made a few casual friends in San Fran who I could've caught up with, but instead, I watched DVDs, ran to the gym, and had a serious workout. I was running back to my apartment when my cell phone rang, and I stopped, looked at the screen, and hoped it was Georgie. Hers was the only number in my contacts. It was a private number, and I nearly didn't answer. When I did, a man with a gruff voice that I instantly recognized said, "Where are you?"

"Hello, Lieutenant Rafter. Why do you want to know?"

"We need to talk. I'm at your apartment."

"Stay there. I'm nearly home. I'll see you in a few minutes."

He was standing at the entrance dressed in a pair of jeans and a dress shirt hanging loosely over his protruding stomach.

"You look stressed," I said, shaking his hand.

"Let's go inside," he replied, glancing behind him to the street.

I noticed that there wasn't a black and white parked anywhere. "Follow me."

As I opened the door, he said, "Jesus, how can you live in a hovel like this?"

"It's cheap," I said, picking up a fresh towel and mopping the sweat from my face.

"Whatever you're paying, it's too much."

I folded my bed into a sofa, and said, "Sit down, and when you've finished with the insults, you might tell me why I'm privileged enough to get a Saturday visit."

"It's personal. Were you interviewed by Detectives Lanza and Selwood?"

"Ah, so that's what this is about. Let me tell you, they're not friends of yours."

"I know that. What did they ask you?"

"It wasn't so much what they asked me, but what they wanted me to say."

"Which was?"

"That you said it was okay for me to go out on the ledge, and that you gave the shooter the order to fire."

"Bastards! What did you say?"

"I told them I shoved you out of the way, and that you never stopped talking to Mr. Evert, so you couldn't have given the order to shoot. If you had, I would've heard, and I didn't."

"Thanks," Rafter said, breathing a sigh of relief.

"Why have they got it in for you?"

"I don't think they have. I've never met or had anything to do with them, but there's a vigilante element in the force, and I suspect they're trying to protect one of their own. Vicki and I are just collateral damage. I'd love to turn the tables on them and get them out of the force. They make it hard for honest cops to do their job."

"The shooter, Pen–," I said, and stopped. "Shit, I nearly forgot. They want me to change my statement."

"That goes without saying. Keep talking."

"Sorry, I can't remember where I was."

"You were about to say something about Penske," Rafter said. "How do you know his name? It hasn't been in the media."

My ploy had worked, and I had the shooter's name. "Ah, yeah Penske. One of the detectives let it drop when he was interviewing me. What's his first name?"

"I shouldn't tell you, but it's Carl."

"I think I had a visit from him and two of his mates last night. Has he got red hair?"

"Yes. Jesus, what did he want?"

"He didn't like the answers I gave Lanza and Selwood. He tried to persuade me to change my mind." I grinned.

"I don't know what you're smiling about. He's got a short fuse, and he's had run-ins with a few of the SWAT guys in the gym. He made an awful mess of them. Did he threaten you?"

"I ran. One of them took a warning shot at me. It missed by a mile. They were sending me a message."

"Unbelievable. Why didn't you call the police?"

I laughed. "They are the police. While we're on the subject, why don't you report Lanza and Selwood to the higher-ups in the force?"

Rafter bit his lip and looked at his shoes. "I can't. I don't know who I can trust. I don't know how high the vigilante element goes."

"And you wanted me to call the police?"

"Sorry, I wasn't thinking. You need to be careful. Can you change your address? Stay at a friend's house until it blows over? Penske's a brute, and I wouldn't put it past him to rough you up. Take my word for it, he's dangerous," Rafter said, getting to his feet.

I opened the door, and said, "Don't worry about me, Lieutenant. I can look after myself."

He was still shaking his head as he walked down the stairs.

Chapter 12

MY PHONE STARTED RINGING at 5:30 a.m. on Monday morning, and I put my head under the pillow and tried to shut it out. Five minutes later my cell phone, which was on a small table next to the bed, started to ring. I rolled over, grabbed it and muttered, "Yeah."

"Josh, it's Paul Wiese. Have you seen the news?"

"I'm still in bed, Mr. Wiese," I replied. "What's so important?"

"You better turn it on. CBS New York broke a story this morning about your disappearance and war record. You're on every channel, and if reporters aren't already at your door, they're soon going to be. I'm guessing they're not going to let you slip out the window this time."

"Thanks," I said, silently cursing.

"Call me after you've watched it," Wiese said.

I put my cell phone on silent and took the landline off the hook. My worst fears had been realized. I turned the television on, and the newscasters were just returning from an ad break. I groaned when I saw a large pic of my face behind them. "This is a sensational story, Kathy."

"It sure is, Warren. It seems there's a lot more to modest hero, Josh Kennelly, than meets the eye. He did two tours in Afghanistan where he was one of only twenty recipients to win our highest wartime award for bravery, the Medal of Honor. He also served with distinction in Iraq."

"Not to say anything of a Purple Heart and Silver Star. I've spoken to soldiers who served with him, and they say if he hadn't had an attitude problem, he would've been one of the very few soldiers ever to have been awarded a second Medal of Honor. His nickname, which he hated, was the Baby-Faced Assassin. It's reputed that he killed more than fifty of the enemy."

A replay of me trying to get Toby Evert and Kirsty off the ledge appeared on the screen. "No wonder he looked fearless on that ledge," Kathy said, "he must have ice running through his veins."

"Yes, Kathy, and there's a lot more to this story than meets the eye. The President presents the Medal of Honor to recipients, but such is this young man's hate of publicity, he didn't go to the White House."

"That's not all, Warren. His real name is Chad Decker, and he's from the small town of Floydada in Texas. Two years ago, he disappeared without a trace and turned up in San Francisco using the name, Josh Kennelly. Six months later, a small firm of lawyers filed on his behalf in the Superior Court to formalize his name change."

"What an amazing story. It's hard to believe. He looks so innocent, which just proves looks can deceive. We've got a crew on their way to his home, and we hope to bring you a live interview with our reluctant hero within the hour. Stay with us, folks, while we take a station break. When we come back, we'll be going live to Floydada."

I heard thumping on my door, and I shouted, "Give me half an hour, and I'll be out to talk to you."

Someone said, "Sure, and just so you know, we're watching your bathroom window."

I was screwed.

I recognized Ernie Post, the proprietor of Ernie's Fishing and Recreation when he appeared on the screen. He was chewing gum and standing next to a reporter who was young enough to be his granddaughter. "What can you tell us about Chad Decker?" she asked.

"Well, his daddy used to brang him in here. They'd buy their bullets, boots, and tackle. Fred and Leonie Decker were as poor as church mice, but they brang young Chad up the right way."

"What was Chad like?"

"He was quiet. Kept to himself. They lived on a small spread a long way from anyone else. One thing though, he was a crack shot, and he'd killed and skinned wild boar and deer before he was ten. They worked hard, and he and his daddy's only pleasures were huntin' and fishin'. He was good at both, real good."

"His parents died while he was still very young. What happened to him? Did he have any relatives to take him in?"

"Only an uncle. Tom Denton. But ol' Tom was pretty sick himself at the time and in no condition tuh look after Chad. At least, that's what he said." Ernie grinned. "Tom's not real sociable if you know what I mean."

"Poor kid. What happened?"

"Henry Nelson was the family's accountant and a close friend. He often went shootin' and fishin' with 'em. Henry just kinda unofficially adopted him. Chad lived with Henry and worked for him in his office. When Chad turned eighteen, Henry talked him intuh joinin' the army. Said it'd be the makin' of him and it was."

"Is Mr. Nelson still in town?"

"Ma'am, sadly Henry had a heart attack and died while Chad was on his first tour of duty in Iraq. He flew back for the funeral. I ain't never seen anyone so broken up."

"Chad sure saw a lot of death in his young years."

"That he did."

"I guess, after he joined the army, you didn't see much of him?"

"That's right, but he used to come back here on furlough. He had a sweet little girlfriend, Susan Miller. She was real purtee. We thought they'd end up gettin' hitched, but it wasn't tuh be."

"What happened?"

"I dunno. No one does. When Chad quit the army and came back about three years ago, we all knew of his war exploits. He was as popular as a rock star, and the townsfolk treated him real well. Wouldn't let him pay for a meal or a drink. When he came here, I refused tuh accept payment for anythin'. After all, how many towns this size produce a genuine, full-blown war hero? We treated him like a king. Then one mornin' he was gone, disappeared. Folks say that he had a dreadful row with Susie the night before, and maybe he left because he had a broken heart. Within a year of him disappearin', she'd married Bill Travers."

"Thank you, Ernie. That's all we have from Floydada," the young reporter said.

"Don't leave us, folks. When we come back, we hope to have Josh Kennelly live, or should that be Chad Decker?" Warren Baxter said. "We'll find out soon enough."

Chapter 13

THE SHOWER BEAT DOWN on me, and I wondered what I was going to tell the media. I had dreaded this day.

I had no idea how many of the enemy I had killed. I did know I'd killed at least three more than was on my record, and they would never appear on any document. I had killed by rifle, pistol, grenade, knife, and on more than one occasion with my bare hands. The army's head shrinkers had examined me and used words like psychopath and sociopath. I was neither. I knew no fear and had a remarkable ability to block out any thoughts or images of those who I had killed. I had read about Custer and Patton and knew, that like them, I had been born without the fear gene. I felt embarrassed and undeserving when I was decorated for my supposed courage. I watched many men who were scared senseless perform the most incredible acts of bravery. I never felt fear, never thought I was going to be killed, and didn't believe I had been brave. Later, I watched brave men return to civilian life and suffer the horrors of post-traumatic stress syndrome while I sailed through unaffected.

I was also examined by the military's medical doctors who were amazed that I had a resting heart rate of only forty. More remarkably in times of stress and extreme danger, my heart rate would drop to thirty. The doctors were fascinated and said this was totally abnormal.

I was promoted twice and demoted twice. The army's assessment was that I was a loner and not a leader. I found this amusing because many of the men volunteered to go on patrol with me, knowing that it increased their probability of getting back to base. I led many attacks on the enemy even though I had no stripes.

I hated my nickname, but, as my reputation and decorations grew, officers and NCOs deferred to me. I didn't like the medals, but in terms of earning respect, they were far more important than any promotion.

My adoptive parents showed me little in the way of love, but my father taught me to hunt and fish. He also taught me never to waste a bullet. Often, I would get into a position upwind and wait for hours without moving until I had a deer or turkey in my sights. It sounds ridiculous, but I can't remember a time when I missed. Not one! The only compliment my father ever gave me was to tell me that I had eyes like a hawk. I would later use the same skills in the army where the prey were the Taliban and al Qaeda.

After my parents had passed away, old Henry Nelson took me in. He was kind and the first and only person who ever loved me. He purposely used big words to force me to use a dictionary, and he made me do the puzzles in the newspapers. He made me think and use my brains, something I'd be forever grateful for. I ran errands for him, did the banking, posted the mail, and he taught me the basics of accounting and how to do simple tax returns. I had one skill that Henry said was unique. I had an uncanny ability to memorize numbers. Henry and I became close friends. Clients would ask him for investment advice, and although I was sure he wasn't licensed to provide it, he'd respond, "Look, if you don't have any debts and have a bit of loose money, you could do a lot worse than buying some shares in Wells Fargo, GE or Caterpillar." I was devastated when I heard of his death. I cried for hours, something that I hadn't done before or since.

Susie Miller was a feisty, green-eyed, brunette with a body that drove men mad. We started fooling around after I turned eighteen, just before I joined the army. She was a young male's dream and my introduction to sex. We became something of an item around the town, and while I loved the sex, I didn't know whether I loved her. My only experience of love were my feelings for Henry Nelson, but Susie was a young woman, and I really had no idea what love between a man and woman was. After I was discharged, we were inseparable, and there was an expectation that we'd get hitched. Then things began to fall apart. The problem was that she loved the free meals, the free drinks, and the adulation that comes with being the girlfriend of one of America's most ruthlessly efficient killers. Someone would buy us a drink and then want to know the gory details of my first kill or how I'd used my knife. I hated it. I couldn't go anywhere without being recognized. Susie loved it, thinking that it made her somebody. She didn't have to put up with the young drunks who wanted to fight me in the hope that a victory would enhance their reputations. The night before I disappeared we had a terrible fight, and I told her I'd be gone in the morning. She told me to go to hell. After a week in San Francisco, I had virtually forgotten her, and I finally had an answer to my burning question.

I still didn't know what love was, but I knew I didn't love Susie.

My discharge from the army was sudden and unexpected. I was in the second vehicle of a small convoy of all-terrain vehicles patrolling the Helmand province in Afghanistan when the lead vehicle was blown apart by an improvised explosive device. I saw the glint of a rifle or binoculars in the mountains, leaped to the ground, and took off up the steep terrain. I had my assault rifle, knife, and a few grenades. I could hear my CO shouting at me to stop, but I never looked back. There was movement on the mountain, and I could see a raghead scurrying away about six hundred yards in front of me. I was gaining on him, and I reached the crest just in time to see him run into a cave. Some of the caves the Taliban hid in had two entrances, and if that were the case, I had lost him. I reached the entrance of the cave and rolled a grenade into it. After the explosion, I didn't hear anything. I waited a minute and then pulled the pin from a second grenade and hurled it deep into the cave. When the dust cleared, I edged my way slowly through the rubble. I'd covered about twenty yards when I saw the raghead. His body had been ripped apart. Then I saw what I thought was a second motionless raghead another five yards further on. I rolled him over. He was a young boy maybe six years old and next to him was another slightly older boy. They were virtually unmarked but very dead. I vomited and choked uncontrollably. I'd never felt so sick, but there was nothing I could do for them. I covered their little bodies in stones in the form of graves. The stupid raghead who had planted the IED must have been their father. He must have thought no one would see him, and he'd have time to escape. He hadn't counted on me. I left the cave and worked my way back to my patrol. For the first time, I couldn't block out the images of those I had killed. The faces of those two little boys were embedded in my mind.

My CO read me the riot act about disobeying orders. I was distraught, the faces of those poor little kids vivid in my mind. I managed to blurt out that I hadn't heard him, the IED having made me temporarily deaf. He'd heard the grenade blasts and asked me if I had killed anyone. I said no. Only God and I would be witnesses to my last mission.

A week later I sought a discharge from the army. The brass tried to talk me out of it, but I had finished with killing. I knew my record was such that my request would be granted.

I have an incredibly strong mind, but even now I still can't totally block out the faces of those kids. I'd learned from the head shrinkers that PTSD is when fear and self-preservation keep flooding your body with adrenaline for the slightest reason long after the battle is over. I knew it wasn't PTSD. I knew no fear. Ever. But I was lost in the tragedy that I had taken two young lives long before their time.

Chapter 14

I THREW MY HOODIE over my shoulder and braced myself. The din outside my door sounded like a baseball crowd. I pushed it open and was stunned. There were reporters and cameras everywhere. Microphones were shoved in my face, and I was besieged with questions. Why had I become a recluse? Why was I hiding? Why hadn't I attended the White House to receive the Medal of Honor? Why hadn't I been back to Floydada? Had I really been called the Baby-Faced Assassin?

The last question stung. I hated that nickname. I told the reporter that no one had ever used it to my face. That wasn't true, but after I'd expressed my displeasure the first few times I heard it, no one in the forces said it to my face. Unfortunately, it was the only name they used behind my back. I spent thirty minutes answering the media's questions as best I could, and some of the reporters finally started to drift away. I apologized to those remaining and said that I had to get to work.

As I pushed my way past them, I saw a pretty young reporter staring into a CBS camera, saying, "This is an amazing story. Chad Decker aka the Baby-Faced Assassin aka Josh Kennelly is so sweet, self-effacing, and modest in real life. It's hard to believe that someone who looks so young and innocent could have killed fifty-four of the enemy on four missions to the Middle East. This reluctant hero may have never been unearthed had it not been for the tragedy that occurred in San Francisco's business district last Monday."

Once I got clear of the reporters, I put my hoodie on and pulled the hood over my head. I walked briskly with my hands in my pockets and my head down. It was nearly 10:30 a.m. when I reached the office, and I wondered whether I still had a job. The receptionist gave me a strange look. "Mr. Eisler said that you're to go straight to his office."

"Thanks," I said, silently cursing. In the pandemonium of the past week, I'd forgotten about Kirsty. I made a mental note to visit her.

I entered Barbara's office, and she looked at me apprehensively. There were no smart comments or sassiness. "Hello, Josh," she said, "please follow me."

Eisler jumped up and shook my hand like we were long lost buddies. "A war hero," he said. "They say you killed fifty-four. Is that true? God, I can't believe it. You look so squeaky clean, so innocent, and yet you're a ruthless killer. Why didn't you tell us?"

"The media exaggerate," I replied. "I'm not a hero or a killer."

"Yeah, yeah." Eisler smirked. "Why did they call you the Baby-Faced Assassin then?"

I felt myself turning red. "No one ever said it to my face. I hate that name. It's a beat-up. I'd appreciate it if you didn't use it, Mr. Eisler."

"Simon, Simon," Eisler said. "Come on, it can't be that hard to call me Simon."

Paul Wiese was sitting at the coffee table. He was staring at me. I'd seen the look many times before. His face was clouded in doubt, and I knew what he was thinking. How could someone as quiet and timid as me have done the things that had been reported in the media? "You're full of surprises, Josh," he said. "Take a seat. We want to discuss your future."

I smiled. "You were going to fire me on Friday after I messed up the shooting of the advertisements. Why the change of mind?"

"Josh, Josh, Josh," Eisler said, "we'd never dream of firing you, and we couldn't care less about those advertisements. We got all the publicity we could wish for this morning, and it's far from finished. It has saved us a small fortune."

"That's right," Wiese added. "Josh, the phones have been running hot this morning with clients who want to have lunch or dinner with you."

"Not to say anything of potential clients who are prepared to switch their business to us, providing you handle their accounts," Eisler said.

"I don't know anything about investments, and I'm not an investment adviser."

"You don't need to be," Eisler said. "You'll have an office next to Paul's, and you'll sit in on meetings with clients and go out to lunch or dinner with them. They just want to touch you, talk to you, have some selfies taken with you. I told you I'd double your salary. That offer's off the table. I'll treble it. Shift your personal stuff into the office next to Paul's today and be ready to start your new career in the morning. This weekend try and find somewhere half decent to live."

"I need to think about it."

"No, you don't, Josh. Your only reservation was the advertising. We've removed that. Don't you like money or, more importantly, don't you trust us?" Eisler asked.

I was screwed. They were going to use me as a sideshow monkey, and if it weren't for Georgie, I would've told them where they could shove their job. If I were going to help her though, I needed to remain employed by Summit. "You're right," I said. "I'm just worried that I don't have any qualifications to advise on investing."

Eisler put his hand on my shoulder. "Don't worry. Paul and I will look after you. You'll be amazed by what you learn. Now, why don't you start packing your stuff?"

I stood up. Their reactions had been what I expected. Wiese was wary, almost scared, and he would never again talk to me like he had on Friday. Eisler couldn't believe what he'd heard about my war record. He wasn't intimidated in the slightest, confident I posed no physical threat to him. Given the opportunity, he would try and prove it. Their vastly differing attitudes were a microcosm of society and one of the reasons I so craved privacy.

When I got to my cubicle, there were more than a hundred messages on my desk. I flicked through them. Most were from clients, but half a dozen were from PR firms wanting me to sign up with them. I'd been through the PR nightmare when I'd first returned from the Middle East. They'd wanted to manage me, organize after-dinner speaking gigs, product endorsements, advertising and even political meetings. I wanted none of it then, and I wanted none of it now. I had written myself a reminder to visit Kirsty which I screwed up and threw in the bin. I'd visit her tonight. My cell phone's message bank was full, and I quickly skimmed through it before deleting all the messages. I had only locked in one name, and she hadn't called.

I sorted out the tax files I was working on and left a note on each one about its status and what was needed to complete it. I had nothing personal in my cubicle, and all I packed were a few pens, my laptop, and two notepads. I was about to leave my cubicle hideaway for the last time when my cell phone rang, and my heart beat a little faster.

"Hi, Georgie," I said, "I was just thinking about you."

"Hello, Josh or do you prefer Chad?" she asked.

"Chad is dead. He's not part of my life."

There was a long pause. "It must have been terrible," she said. "It's been on television the whole day. There are crews in Floydada, and they've interviewed some of your old army buddies. You're very brave."

There was that word again. If she knew the truth, she wouldn't be thinking that. "How much longer are you here for, Georgie?"

"I have two months accumulated leave. I'm taking all of it. The lawyers for dad's estate are dealing with some company in Shanghai and getting nowhere. Worse, the bank has intensified its threats to foreclose on the house. I've managed to stall them by making some payments, but we're still in default."

"I'm sorry I haven't found anything."

"I didn't expect you would have after what you've been through. I wasn't calling for a report." She laughed. "Josh, I thought I might have heard from you over the weekend. Would you like to catch up for coffee or dinner?"

"I'd love to. I know a nice little restaurant in Union Square."

Again, the phone went quiet. "I don't think you're going to be able to go anywhere in this city for quite a while without being mobbed. I thought you might enjoy a home cooked meal with Mom and me."

"That sounds great," I said.

We made a date for Friday night. I was already counting down the hours.

Chapter 15

I ENTERED THE JIMMY Carter Memorial Hospital, and before I could even ask about Kirsty, the nurses behind the reception counter were telling me how brave I was. Then they cooed about how beautiful the roses I was carrying were. This was the reason I had left Floydada, and for two years, I had enjoyed total anonymity in San Francisco. Fate had dealt me a bad hand that day on the ledge, and now I was experiencing what I had in Floydada multiplied by a hundred. I admonished myself as I walked down the corridor to Kirsty's room. Here I was moaning about having no privacy when a good man had lost his life.

I was surprised that Kirsty was still in hospital as she had suffered no physical injuries. She was watching television, and her face lit up when she saw me. "Josh," she said, "it's so good of you to come and see me. I've been watching you on television all day. It doesn't matter what channel I flick to, there you are."

She was smiling, but her skin was a sickly white, and she looked thinner. I kissed her on the cheek, and said, "I'm sorry I haven't been able to visit earlier. I've been snowed under. Where can I put these?"

"Oh, they're exquisité," she said taking the roses from me and breathing in their fragrance. "Don't apologize. You must have had everyone and their dogs wanting to talk to you. Had it not been for you, I wouldn't be here now. I don't know how to thank you."

"You flatter me. I'm sure Lieutenant Rafter would have gotten you to safety."

"No, he wouldn't have. He and Vicki visited me the day after, and they were in again on the weekend. He said that, if you hadn't been there, Evert wouldn't have made it back to the window. I owe you my life."

"If you insist. Thanks."

"Josh, I saw your interview where you called Evert a good man. I don't think he was a good man. I hate him, and I'm glad he's dead. I'm sorry if that offends you," Kirsty said visibly shaking.

I took one of her hands in mine and massaged it, saying, "What you went through was terrible, Kirsty. I can understand your feelings. How long before you're allowed to go home?"

"Soon, I hope. I've been having terrible nightmares, and the flashbacks come when I least expect them. I can't stop myself screaming, and when the nurses come, I feel so stupid."

I didn't know what civilians called it, but she was suffering PTSD. That accounted for why she looked so unwell. I wondered whether the police had added to her stress. "Did Lieutenant Rafter and Officer Enright ask you any questions?"

"None. They're so kind and brought me chocolates and flowers. All they were worried about was my recovery. They're lovely, not like those other pigs."

"What?"

"Two detectives visited me the day after. They were nasty and tried to get me to say that I had heard Lieutenant Rafter say fire or shoot. I told them I couldn't remember anything, which is true, and they got angry with me. The young one was a real sleaze."

"Detectives Lanza and Selwood," I said.

"Yes, did they interview you? They tried to convince me that the shooter, who they wouldn't name, had saved my life. That's when I got angry and told them it was you who had saved my life. What are they doing?"

"Yeah, they interviewed me too. There was no reason for the officer to shoot and by doing so, he put your life at risk. I suspect the District Attorney's looking at pressing charges, and if he doesn't now, he will after the Coronial Inquest. I think Lanza and Selwood are trying to cover his ass. All you have to do is tell the truth. Don't be swayed by anyone else, leastwise Lanza and Selwood."

"Has anyone else from the office visited you."

"The girls have been in every day. Oh, and I nearly forgot, Mr. Wiese, came in on the weekend."

"Paul Wiese? That's surprising."

"Yes, I thought the same. It was uncomfortable, and the conversation was stilted. He seemed to be suggesting that Simon Eisler had never refused to meet with Evert. I told him that Barbara Sumner had been adamant that there was no way Mr. Eisler was meeting or talking to Evert. Then he had the audacity to ask me if I were sure."

"What did you say?"

"I said that I was in the hospital because of the stress, not because I'd had a lobotomy."

I laughed. I hadn't realized that Kirsty had a feisty streak. "How did he respond?"

"He didn't, and he left a few minutes later."

"Talking about leaving, I better get going," I said, kissing her on the forehead. "Let's hope they let you go home tomorrow."

As I walked out of the hospital to be greeted by a bitterly cold night, all I could think about was the ass covering that was going on. Elements of the SFPD were going out of their way to make sure the shooter never faced justice. For some reason, Eisler had sent Wiese to convince Kirsty that she should change her mind, or perhaps they were hoping the trauma might have resulted in memory loss. I didn't understand. Eisler had refused to see or talk to Evert — it was no big deal. CEOs, army officers, politicians, and others engrossed in their own self-importance did it every day. Why was he trying to hide it? It might be rude, but it wasn't a crime.

Chapter 16

IT DIDN'T TAKE LONG to find out what my new job entailed. I was definitely the monkey and Eisler, and Wiese were the organ grinders. I was introduced to clients who fawned over and were more than a little in awe of me. They gushed over my achievements and wanted to talk about conditions in Iraq and Afghanistan. I had been worried they would ask me about the killing and violence and was pleasantly surprised when they didn't. Those questions would come much later, and usually after an alcohol enhanced lunch or dinner. A few clients who'd asked to meet me were standoffish, and like Simon Eisler, were surprised and clearly not impressed or even slightly overawed by what they saw.

Paul Wiese's office was a smaller version of Eisler's, and once the client hard sell began, I was told just to nod and agree. Wiese was smooth and very knowledgeable and could discuss shares, bonds, property, and tax with great authority. However, his main concentration was on the shipping containers and what he described as their tax minimization attraction. I knew a little about taxes but didn't know whether it was a tax deferral scheme, tax avoidance or tax evasion. The only words that Wiese used in relation to taxation were reduce, minimize, defer and the derivations thereof. These were powerful hooks that appealed to clients and made them keen on the container scheme. Wiese explained to clients that Summit could act as an agent to acquire the containers on their behalf and charge a modest three percent commission of the cost. He also told clients that they were free to buy the containers themselves, but they would almost certainly pay more because they didn't have Summit's contacts or buying power. When clients asked about income distributions, he said they could be as low as two percent per quarter and as high as seven percent. If clients wavered after hearing this, he would immediately move back to the tax minimization benefits which in most instances appeased the waverers.

If I were going to be able to help Georgie, I needed to know how the scheme worked so when there was a break between seeing clients, I said, "Mr. Wiese, Paul, what security do our clients have?"

"Haven't you been listening? They own the physical containers. What better security could they have?"

"There are millions of shipping containers," I said. "They're on ships, in container yards, and some are probably in repair shops. How can our clients identify their containers?"

Wiese sighed. "Every shipping container manufactured has to be certified by Lloyds or some other registered body. There's a CSC plate, which stands for container safety convention, on every container. It's got the date of manufacture stamped on it, the CSC safety approval number, and most importantly for our clients, the serial number of the container on their invoice. They can always identify the containers they own."

"If need be, how do they convert the physical containers into cash?"

"Very few ever want to. The returns and tax benefits are too attractive. However, if they did, they have a guarantee from the supplier who will buy them back for the same price our client paid."

"Where is the supplier incorporated?"

"Jeez, you ask a lot of questions," Wiese said, glancing at his watch. "Our next client's here."

Just before 1:00 p.m., we met with a new client who was with us because he specifically wanted to meet me. I knew he was well-heeled because Wiese's PA had booked a fine Italian restaurant, the Acquerello on Sacramento Street, for lunch. As it turned out, the lunch was a complete failure because we were constantly interrupted by patrons wanting to shake my hand. One even asked for my autograph which I sheepishly gave him. The client didn't seem to mind, but Wiese was totally pissed off. After we got back to the offices and the client had left, he said, "That could have cost us important new business. From now on, we'll either dine in private rooms or one of the meeting rooms here. I'm not going through that again."

"But it didn't," I said. "He really liked the container scheme. I still don't understand it. How do we have the expertise to hire out what must be an enormous container fleet?"

"We don't," Wiese replied. "We use agents to make sure that we get maximum fleet utilization."

"I see what you mean about it being a great business. We can pay investors up to seven percent a quarter even after paying agents and taking a healthy management fee. If the market ever gets back to charging pre-GFC rates, our investors will make a fortune." I didn't believe a word of what I'd just said.

"That's right," Wiese said, "you're starting to catch on."

Before the week was over, I had another client lunch and two dinners in the private dining rooms of fancy restaurants. I didn't drink and was a recluse, so dining with half-drunken clients who wanted to know all the gory details of my exploits in the Middle East was testing. Had it not been for Georgie, I would have quit.

I noticed that Wiese was careful to ensure that clients signed consents and documentation relevant to their investments. This documentation went to his PA who created accounts and inputted details into the firm's computer systems. I had not been provided with computer access to client files and had no reason to ask for it. After all, I was just for show. However, I did observe Wiese's PA taking copies of the documents and filing them in newly opened client files that were housed in large steel cabinets adjacent to her desk. I guessed the originals were filed in an external document filing and retrieval facility. Wiese had a set of keys to the cabinets that I knew he kept in the top right-hand drawer of his unlocked desk.

It was opportune that my elevation to the executive suite had resulted in me being given a security swipe card that allowed me to access the building together with the keys to the offices.

Chapter 17

I ARRIVED AT THE office building at 7:00 a.m. Friday and was pleased to see a steady stream of people entering through the revolving door. Summit's offices were still locked, and the lights were turned off. I let myself in, made my way to Paul Wiese's office, and took the ring of cabinet keys from his desk. I quickly opened the cabinet with the drawer marked A –E. The files were in clearly marked suspension folders, and I went straight to the one labeled Tobias Evert. It was empty. I took out the file in front of it for Harold Eckhart and quickly perused it. The amount of detail that it contained was comprehensive and included detailed statements of income and position together with a risk profile. In addition, there were personal and contact details for Eckhart, his wife, and children. I was impressed by the content and wondered where Evert's file was, and what it would reveal. Perhaps it was with the firm's lawyers, and if that were the case, I was screwed. Alternatively, given the gravity of the situation, Simon Eisler may have taken it into his possession. Either way, I would have nothing to tell Georgie tonight.

I opened a bottle of mineral water and sat behind my desk pondering my next move. Twenty minutes later, Paul Wiese did a double take as he walked past my door. "You're early, Josh. We don't have our first appointment until nine. You look worried. What's wrong?"

"Has the Coroner's office contacted you?" I asked.

Wiese scratched his head. "No, why would they? If you remember correctly, that madman cleared the floor. You were the only one he let stay. I didn't see anything."

"No, but you were there when Evert took Kirsty hostage. Plus, you were Mr. Evert's financial adviser. I thought they'd want to ask you about his financial position."

"I wasn't his financial adviser. Simon met him on a flight to LA and provided the initial advice. As you know, Simon's the firm's rainmaker, and our modus operandi is that he wins the clients, and I service them. We tried it with Evert, but he insisted on being advised by Simon. I only met him twice, and all he could talk about was the deals Simon had put him into. We tried, but he didn't want me advising him and made no attempt to hide it."

"He was one of Simon's clients?"

"One of the very few. Josh, you don't have to worry about the inquest. You were heroic. I'll let Simon know the Coroner's office might be in touch," Wiese said as he went into his office.

"Thanks," I muttered. I now knew Evert's file was most likely in Simon Eisler's office.

I spent most of the day having my hand vigorously shaken and being patted on the back by new clients. I then listened in silence to Paul Wiese's spin about shipping containers again. The only relief came from my thoughts about seeing Georgie. Wiese was a persuasive salesman, and in three meetings, I heard clients commit to investing over five million dollars. I knew enough about human nature to know that someone was making big bucks, and it wasn't the firm's clients. Our last meeting finished just before 5:00 p.m., and I was out the door like lightning.

I quickly showered and shaved and then applied a liberal quantity of Opium, the only aftershave I owned. While I wasn't into fashion, I scrubbed up okay in a smart navy blue, waterproof jacket, a light blue shirt, beige pleated sports pants and matching loafers. I checked myself out in the mirror and called a cab.

By the time we crossed the bridge, the fog was starting to come in, and I hoped I wouldn't find myself stranded in a few hours' time. The exterior of the house was rustic, dark timber, and it overlooked the bay. The butterflies in my stomach were rampaging as I rang the old brass doorbell. Georgie opened the door. She was wearing jeans and a loose-fitting blue and white top. She greeted me with a kiss on the cheek, and I could feel my heart pounding. At that moment, I wished I'd bought flowers, but I was rusty. I hadn't had a date for a long time. The house was warm, and there were huge colorful rugs thrown over the wooden floor.

"Mom's cooking," she said, taking my hand and leading me out to the kitchen.

Her mother was small and petite and didn't seem to have changed much from the family photo that I had seen. She was still wearing a bindi in the middle of her forehead, and while she hadn't aged, I could see the stress on her face. "I'm so sorry for your loss, Mrs. Evert," I said.

"He was a good man. For more than thirty years, we used to stand here, talk about the day's events, and enjoy the bay. I would wash, and he would dry. It's funny. You don't miss the small things until they're gone."

I didn't know what to say. Georgie squeezed my hand and said, "We miss him so much."

"Thank you for trying to save him, Josh. You were very brave," Mrs. Evert said. "Can I get you something to drink?"

"I'm fine, thanks."

I felt a tugging on my hand. "I want to show you the views from the balcony before we're enveloped in fog," Georgie said.

There was a chill in the air, and I put my arm around Georgie's waist. It seemed so natural.

Dinner was porterhouse, baked potatoes, mushrooms, onions, and spinach. "Georgina wanted me to prepare a seafood curry, but I thought a boy from Texas would enjoy a steak."

"I'm hardly a boy." I laughed. "The steak is superb, but I'm sure I would have enjoyed your curry."

"Next time," Mrs. Evert said.

"I wonder how a good old boy from Texas will handle a spicy Indian curry." Georgie laughed.

By the time Mrs. Evert served caramel apple pie, I felt like I'd known her for ages. Like her daughter, she was warm and friendly. They rejoiced Toby's life and relived and laughed about the good times they had shared. Occasionally, they became maudlin, but it was only fleeting. On a more serious note, Georgie told me they'd received a demand from the Bank of America for a credit card debt in excess of a hundred thousand dollars. Mrs. Evert had had no idea that the card existed and dreaded opening the daily mail. Clearly, Toby had been living on the financial edge. We moved into the living room for coffee and continued a very enjoyable night. Neither of them raised or asked me any questions about my war record. Just after 10:00

p.m., Mrs. Evert said she was going to bed and wished me goodnight.

Georgie turned the television on and sat down on the sofa next to me. Before she could ask, I said, "I'm sorry, I haven't been able to find anything. I don't have computer access, and your father's file wasn't where I thought it'd be."

"I wasn't going to ask. I know that if you'd found something you would have told me," she said. "I want to know why you told me you were a nothing when you're a highly-decorated war hero."

"What I did in the war is not something I care to talk about."

"I know. You wouldn't have changed your name and gone into hiding, had that not been the case. I want to know why you were so anxious to portray yourself as a loser. It's not very attractive, you know."

"Habit I guess."

"Well, I didn't believe a word of what you said." Georgie laughed, curling her feet up under herself as she placed her hand on my forearm. "I'm a very good judge of character, and I knew there was far more to you than you were making out."

My heart was beating hard again, and I was stuck for words. I blurted out, "I intend to find out what happened with your father. It just might take a little longer than I thought."

"You don't like talking about yourself." She smiled. "That will change with time. It will be great if you can help with dad, but I don't want you to think that you have to have something to report before calling me."

Her face was close to mine, and I gently kissed her. "It's been over two years since I kissed anyone." I laughed, embarrassed.

"Welcome back to normality," she said. "Sorry, I'd like to talk and snuggle all night, but I have to be up early."

I apologized and called a cab. Thirty minutes later when I was leaving, we kissed again, and our tongues interlocked in a passionate exchange. I wanted to linger, but Georgie pushed me gently away.

"Your cab's here," she said. "Why don't we catch a movie tomorrow night? If we get there a few minutes late, it'll be dark, and you won't be mobbed."

I'd always had amazing self-control, but emotions I'd never experienced before were running amok. I sat in the cab wondering whether it was possible to fall in love so quickly. I'd never felt this way about Susie.

Chapter 18

WE WENT TO THE movies on Saturday, and on Sunday, Georgie took me out to Alcatraz. I'd been in San Francisco for nearly two years, and it was something I'd been meaning to do, but had never gotten around to it. A few people pointed at us, and I felt others looking, but no one approached me to shake my hand.

Perhaps they were looking at Georgie? She was vibrant, full of life and talked a lot which suited me just fine because it was something I didn't like to do. I told her about the family photo that I'd seen.

She shrieked. "The one where I was wearing the big glasses, had buck teeth, and my hair was in braids."

"That's the one." I laughed.

"No," she said. "I'd just played the dork in a school play, and everything was fake. My dad thought it'd be funny if we got a family pic while I was still made up."

"I thought it was the transformation from duckling to swan."

"Ugly duckling you mean," she said, punching me in the arm.

It felt like I'd known her for years, and I wondered whether this was what love was like.

On the boat on the way back from Alcatraz, we arranged to have dinner at one of the restaurants around Union Square on Wednesday night. Things were moving fast. After Georgie was in a cab on the way to Sausalito, I turned my mind to her father. I was way out of my depth. I'm sure that there were those far cleverer than me who would've had no difficulty hacking into the firm's computer systems. I was reliant on looking at documents, and even then, there was no certainty I'd understand them. I asked myself if Georgie had been George, would I be trying to be so helpful? I wasn't without conscience.

I arrived at the offices on Monday morning, resolved to find Mr. Evert's file and ascertain what had occurred between him and the firm. I knew the all-important file was most likely in the custody of Simon Eisler or Barbara Sumner. When I was certain that Eisler had gone out, I made my way down to his office only to be told by Barbara that he wasn't available. I asked her how long he would be, while I checked the security and layout of her office. A four-drawer locked walnut filing cabinet sat behind her matching desk. I also noticed key holes on her desk drawers, and I got the feeling that everything would be locked when she wasn't there.

"What do you want to see him about?" she asked.

"I want to know what I have to do to become a registered investment adviser."

"You'd be better off asking Paul about that."

"Do you have any applications forms?" I asked, looking at the filing cabinet.

"No, I don't. Talk to Paul."

"Thanks," I said. I'd learned nothing.

The rest of that day and most of the next, I kept an inconspicuous eye on the chief executive's office suite and found that it was never unattended. Either Eisler or Barbara were always there, and I had no opportunity to do any snooping. By Wednesday morning I was becoming desperate. I walked down the corridor and was in front of one of the interview rooms when I heard raised voices, and Eisler say, "It's not my problem, and I don't see why it's such a big deal."

The drapes were drawn, and I couldn't see who else was in the room, and then I heard the unmistakable voice of Detective Lanza. "It's a big deal because the media are making such a fuss about it. The *Chronicle's* running a front-page article tomorrow comparing the SFPD with Wyatt Earp and Doc Holliday. There's an election coming up, and the Mayor wants heads to roll. We want to make sure they're the right heads."

I walked past the office and bent down to slowly tie my shoe laces. What were they talking about? What had Lanza meant by the right heads?

"Yeah. We don't care about those pussy negotiators," Selwood said. "They just get in the way. More trouble than they're worth. If we lost a few of them, the SWAT team would be far more effective."

"You might have gotten Kirsty to say that Rafter gave the order to fire if you hadn't put so much pressure on her," Wiese said. "You were too heavy handed."

"Jesus, Paul. You can't talk. She's in shock, her brain is addled, and you couldn't even convince her to say that I hadn't refused to see or talk to that dopey prick," Eisler said.

"If we can get the kid to change his mind about what he heard we can sweep all of this under the carpet," Lanza said. "He not only saved the girl, but he's also a war hero and Medal of Honor winner. He's got credibility and, even if he says he can't be sure, but Rafter might have given the order to fire, SWAT and our man, are off the hook."

"The lunatic was about to drive a knife into her. The officer's the one who should be getting a medal," Eisler said.

"You couldn't get Kennelly to change his mind last time you spoke to him. What makes you think you can now?" Wiese asked.

"We spoke to him here. When we interview him again, we're going to do it downtown. It won't be anywhere near as pleasant," Lanza replied.

"Didn't you read his war record?" Eisler snapped. "How are you going to break him?"

"We can be very persuasive. We have our ways," Selwood responded.

I'd gotten so caught up in the conversation that I hadn't seen one of the investment advisers walk past me, and wasn't paying any attention when she returned a few minutes later. "Josh, are you all right?" she asked.

"I'm fine," I said, quickly standing up. "Just a little dizzy spell. Nothing to worry about."

"You've been through a lot," she said. "Take it easy. Don't overdo it."

"Thanks, I won't."

As I walked away, I could still hear muffled voices. I was confused. It was obvious that the two detectives were doing everything they could to protect Officer Penske and SWAT, but why were Eisler and Wiese involved?

It was no surprise when Mandy buzzed me later that morning to say that Detectives Lanza and Selwood were in reception.

I knew what was going to occur and I said, "Good morning, Detectives. Have you been here long?"

Lanza gave me a sly look. "We've just finished interviewing your bosses and would like another word with you."

"Fine."

"Downtown, hero boy," Selwood butted in.

"Oh," I said, feigning surprise. "Did you interview Mr. Eisler and Mr. Wiese downtown?"

"We just want to get you on the record," Lanza said. "It's routine."

"I've already made a statement. Did you get Mr. Eisler and Mr. Wiese on the record?"

"What we did with them is private," Lanza responded, "as is anything you say to us."

"I bet," I muttered.

"What? What did you say?" Selwood said, poking his chest into me. I could tell he didn't think much of me or my wartime exploits. There was always someone wanting to take me down a peg or two.

"Nothing."

"Don't make the mistake of thinking we're as soft as those ragheads. We're not like them. We know how to fight. There are no easy kills here," Selwood snapped.

I could see the carotid artery on the right-hand side of his neck throbbing, and I smiled knowing that, had I wanted to, I could kill him in less than thirty seconds. "You fought in the Middle East?" I asked, knowing he hadn't, because there was nothing soft about the ragheads.

"Nah, I was too busy defending the streets of San Francisco from real killers."

"It's a shame you weren't at my apartment a few nights ago when I was fired at, but then again, I'm sure you know all about that."

"You were fired at?" Lanza asked, fighting back a smirk. "Did you report it to the police?"

"Would they have done anything if I had?"

"Of course. The SFPD always looks after its community-minded citizens."

"More like its own," I said. "When would you like me to come in?"

"You've got such a smart mouth. You're coming with us now." Lanza said. "Don't worry. It'll only be for a couple of hours."

"I'll have to clear it with Mr. Wiese."

"We've already taken care of that. Come on, let's go," Selwood said, nudging me in the back.

Chapter 19

THEY SHOVED ME INTO the back of a Ford and took me to 3rd Street. Not a word was spoken on the short trip, and I couldn't believe the fools were trying to intimidate me. They marched me up the stairs, one on each side as if I were Don Corleone.

I was taken to an interrogation room that could have been one of the props from Law and Order, right down to the one-way mirror. They sat me behind a narrow, four-legged table. Lanza took the chair on the other side of me while Selwood paced around behind me. This was the same building where I'd made my earlier statement in the comparative comfort of Lieutenant Rafter's office.

"We're about to go on record. Do you have any queries before we start?" Lanza asked.

"Do you control the recording equipment?" I responded. "I thought everything was recorded from the time I set foot in this room."

"I think he's questioning your integrity, Matt," Selwood said, putting his hands on my shoulders and squeezing as hard as he could. I had a vision of the heel of my hand striking under his nose and driving the bone through his brain. I shook my head. What was I thinking? I had resolved never to kill again.

"We control the recording equipment," Lanza said, "but once we start, the interview will be continuous."

"What about after hours editing?"

"I'm gonna overlook that comment," Lanza said, "but you'd be wise to keep a civil tongue."

He then went over the formalities about the date, time, and who was present, and the interrogation began. It covered most of what they had previously asked me, until Lanza said, "Why didn't you tell me about your war record?"

"You never asked me."

"More importantly, why did you change your name?"

"Yeah," Selwood said, "what did you do that you're trying to hide?"

"You've obviously watched the interviews on television. I craved privacy and being Chad Decker gave me none."

"We watched them," Selwood said, "but we don't buy your story. No one in San Francisco would've known Chad Decker or what you had done. You didn't need to change your name because of that. What did you really do?"

I sighed loudly. "Everyone in Floydada knew who I was and so did most of Texas. How long do you think it would've taken them to find me, if I'd used my right name? Besides, what's it got to do with Mr. Evert's death?"

Lanza ignored my question. "Let me take you back to last Monday. The wind was howling, it was raining, the helicopters were thumping, and Lieutenant Rafter was barking instructions. There was a lot of other background noise with police on walkie-talkies, cell phones, and laptops. Could he have instructed the SWAT team to fire, and with all the noise, you didn't hear him?"

"No way, and you made a mistake, Detective. He wasn't barking instructions. He was speaking in a calm, measured manner that should have ensured everyone got off that ledge alive. He is blameless," I said.

Selwood was standing directly behind me, and his hands were on my shoulders again. "With all that noise, how can you be certain you heard everything that Lieutenant Rafter said?"

"We were in sync. We were both trying to achieve the same goal. I'm one hundred percent certain that he issued no instructions to the SWAT team. Sorry. That's not right. I did hear one of his officers tell them to prepare to stand down."

Lanza's face was black. That was the last response he had wanted. "You say that you and the Lieutenant were in sync. Is that why he consented to you going out on the ledge?"

"Don't you remember that I told you he never consented? I pushed him out of the way."

"Did he immediately tell you to come back in?" Lanza asked.

"I don't recall."

"You're adamant that Lieutenant Rafter never told the SWAT team to fire, but you can't recall whether he told you to come back inside. Do you have a selective memory?"

I had to admit that Lanza had made a very good point which went straight to my credibility. "Detective, there were plenty of armed police on the sixteenth floor. Lieutenant Rafter could have ordered one of them to fire from close range. Why would he order a ground sniper over two hundred yards away to take a pot shot?"

"Okay, okay," Lanza said, "Let's say that's right. You were on the ledge, and you saw Evert raise the knife. Can you understand why someone two hundred yards away could think the young girl was in grave danger?"

"No, the sights on the rifle he used are so precise that he

would've seen exactly what I saw from a yard away. He was trigger-happy or perhaps something worse."

"Something worse," Selwood said, bending down and putting his face so close to mine that I could feel flecks of spit. "What's that supposed to mean?"

"That's for the Coroner to determine."

Lanza stood up and said, "It's 1:16 p.m. and we're about to pause."

"You said the interview was going to be continuous. Why have you changed your mind?"

"Shut up," Selwood shouted. "You're a lying piece of shit. Rafter told you it was okay to go out on that ledge, and he told the SWAT team to fire. Why are you covering for him? I have a mind to give you a good whupping."

"You wish." I grinned.

Selwood flew at me, but Lanza pinned his arms before he could throw a punch. I was disappointed Lanza had moved so quickly. I smiled and said, "You need to curb your temper before it gets you in trouble."

They left the interrogation room, and a few minutes later, Lanza returned, and said, "You're free to go."

"Are you gonna drive me back to my office?"

"Don't push it," he said.

I bounded down the stairs, happy to see the back of Lanza and Selwood, but none the wiser as to why they had it in for Rafter. It was cold, and I plunged my hands into my pockets only to find my keys were missing. I climbed back up the stairs, but there was no one on the desk so I went to the interrogation room. It was locked. Cursing, I pushed the double doors that I had seen

Lanza go through, and there he was sitting at a desk on the west-side wall. As I walked toward him, he stood up and said, "What the hell. What are you doing back here?"

I could see my photo on the wall with my name below it. I glanced past Lanza. There were also photos of Evert, Rafter, Enright, and a man with distinct red eyebrows and cropped hair — Officer Carl Penske.

Lanza opened the door to the interrogation room, and I retrieved my keys, but my accidental return had yielded much more. It didn't prove Lanza had told Penske what I said, but if he hadn't, why had Penske and two of his goons tried to rough me up? Had Penske been the one who fired at me?

Chapter 20

I PICKED UP A copy of Thursday's *San Francisco Chronicle.* The front page was headlined Police Killing Epidemic, and the article by Hamish Gidley-Baird stated:

The San Francisco Police Department is facing intense criticism and scrutiny after another citizen was killed by an officer.

Anger is mounting in the community about the number of fatal officer-involved shootings. Family man and longtime Sausalito resident, Mr. Tobias Evert, was the latest victim. Mr. Evert was shot and killed by a police sniper eleven days ago. This is the thirteenth officer-involved killing this year and follows the ten lives lost last year. Mr. Evert was distraught and mentally unbalanced when he took a young, female hostage, forcing her onto the ledge of a high-rise building on California Street. Reliable sources have informed your correspondent that police negotiators and returned war hero, Josh Kennelly, had managed to calm Mr. Evert and that the hostage was in no danger. Despite this, Mr. Evert was shot and killed by the San Francisco Police Department's 'supposedly' finest.

Despite there being more than forty, fatal officer-involved shootings in the past five years, no charges were filed against any of the officers. In eighteen cases, the suspects were unarmed. In the case of Mr. Evert, he was holding a knife, but police had calmed him, and he was helping his hostage back to safety. When she stumbled and almost fell from the ledge, Mr. Evert saved her by reaching out and holding her with the hand that was holding the knife. An examination of the video and the angle of the knife shows that he had no intention of using it.

In the past five years, nearly 200 officers, roughly nine percent of the 2,300-strong force, were involved in shootings, and ten of those were involved in more than one. We cannot name the officer who killed Mr. Evert, but we understand this is the third shooting that he has been involved in.

Your correspondent understands that San Francisco County District Attorney, George Calder, is investigating the circumstances that led to Mr. Evert's death and that might lead to the officer and his superiors being charged. A spokesman for DA Calder said, "It's too early to draw conclusions, but the spate of officer-involved shootings is worrying and needs further investigation."

DA Calder went on to say, "The SFPD should adopt a policy requiring officers to respond to physical threats with the minimum necessary force." With respect to the DA, the San Francisco Police Commission has had a policy for years mandating that officers make their best endeavors to de-escalate conflict situations before using force. The problem seems to be that this policy has never been enforced and elements within the SFPD have resisted it. Perhaps if the DA had charged officers involved in killings, those vigilante elements of the SFPD would have curbed their ways, and Mr. Evert would still be alive.

When contacted, Mayor Brady, declined to comment saying that it would be inappropriate given that the matter was still under investigation. The *Chronicle* understands that the Mayor's office has piled the pressure on the DA to complete his investigation and lay charges before the end of the year. With elections next year, and the polls indicating the Mayor has only a wafer-thin margin, your correspondent cannot help but wonder if the DA's investigation has more to do with self-interest than justice.

The last thing the citizens of San Francisco want is to be living in a police county; a county where the police force has set itself up as judge, jury, and executioner. — a police county that has no respect for the rule of law. San Francisco is not Dodge City, and it doesn't need a police force made up of Wyatt Earp and Doc Holliday facsimiles. Vigilante justice is a huge oxymoron.

Of course, the overwhelming majority of police are honest, diligent, brave, and giving. It is the few bad apples that need weeding out, and the DA has an opportunity to draw a line in the sand with the killing of Mr. Evert. For the sake of the county, let's hope he takes it.

The *Chronicle* has undertaken to follow this matter to its culmination and to keep you, our loyal readers, fully informed.

I read the article twice, drawing the conclusion that the journalist, Hamish Gidley-Baird, was either naïve or had a lot of guts — I was almost sure it was the latter.

Chapter 21

HAMISH GIDLEY-BAIRD'S ARTICLE HAD had a big impact on me, and had been on my mind most of the day. I spread it out on my kitchen table and read it again. Was there really a group of cowboys in the SFPD who were taking the law into their own hands? Even if there were, it wasn't my problem, and there was nothing I could do about it. My job was to steer clear of the cops, get Mrs. Evert's money back, and thwart the bank from seizing her house. I knew I wasn't terribly bright, but what I lacked in brains, I made up for with uncanny gut feelings. Sadly, gut feelings wouldn't help Mrs. Evert, and I racked my brain to come up with a solution. If I were a computer whiz, it would've been easy to get the information. On reflection, even someone with only average computer skills could have gotten it. My problem was that my only skill was killing and maiming, and the use of that skill in civilian life was severely limited. Besides, I had resolved never to kill again. I threw the *Chronicle* in the bin, put my fingertips to my forehead and forced myself to think.

After a few minutes, I came up with the idea of working late at the office tomorrow night and snooping, but knew I wouldn't get away with it, and worse, it would look suspicious. My job was to smile, shake hands and say thanks, so there was absolutely no reason for me to work late. Then I had a brainwave. On the way to the office tomorrow morning, I would buy a small flashlight, and when I left to go home, I would leave my jacket hanging on the back of my chair.

I was going to have dinner at Georgie's tomorrow night, and when I called to cancel she didn't try to hide her disappointment. I liked that, and would've loved to have been with her, but I had to find out what trouble her father had gotten himself into. I thought about telling her what I was up to but thought better of it. Instead, I said that Simon Eisler had organized drinks with clients at the office, and I had to be there.

It was 7:30 p.m. when I let myself into the building on the pretext, if anyone saw me, that I'd forgotten my jacket. Fortunately, the office security lights provided more than enough visibility. I locked the doors behind me and made my way down the corridor to Eisler's office. Before entering, I checked the drawers on Barbara's desk and filing cabinet. As expected, they were locked, and there was no sign of keys. Eisler's office was everything Barbara's wasn't. The cabinets and desk drawers were open, and I sat down at his desk. Using the flashlight, I methodically started going through the files in his drawers. They were untidy, disorganized, and after thirty minutes, I had found very little and certainly not Tobias Evert's file. It could mean only one thing; the file was under the care of the efficient Barbara Sumner. I was screwed again, and short of smashing the locks, there was no way I was going to get that file.

As I was pondering my bad luck, the lights in the corridor came on, and I heard voices. I pushed the drawers closed and ducked under Eisler's desk. I heard Barbara say, "Why couldn't we have gone to a motel?"

"Honey, I have to see Paul later tonight. This is more convenient," Eisler said.

"For someone with so much money, you can be a real cheapskate," Barbara replied.

"Don't be like that, Barbara. Come on. Don't be mad. I'm going to make it up to you."

I couldn't see anything, and there was a moment of silence before I heard Barbara groan, "God, I love you."

I heard a thump and could see black stilettoes below the front panel of the desk. Then I saw a black G-string sitting on top of the stilettoes, and the desk started to rock with force. "I love fucking on this desk," Eisler shouted.

"Do you love me, darling?" Barbara gasped.

"Yeah, yeah, of course," Eisler said, and then he let out an almighty yell, and the desk stopped rocking.

"You're a fantastic lover," Barbara moaned.

I could hear Eisler panting like a dog. "Fuck. I needed that," he said.

"When we're living on Hvar, we won't have to skulk around anymore. You know they're calling it the second Cannes. I'm sick of sneaking around and hiding from your wife. It's going to be wonderful once we're in Croatia, isn't it?"

"Yeah, I can hardly wait."

"You can be a cold bastard, Simon. Could you be any less enthusiastic? I'm going to the rest rooms to get cleaned up."

Eisler walked around to the other side of his desk, and I thought he was going to sit down. If he did, he couldn't help but see me. I was perfectly calm, without fear or nerves. If he discovered me and got physical, it would be very painful — for him. He did not sit down, but instead removed a painting from the wall and opened the safe behind it. I had a clear view of the five-number combination. Eisler took out what looked like a black travel agency folder, and put some documents in it, before putting it back in the safe and hurriedly closing it.

I heard Barbara return and say, "I can't wait to get out of this place. I don't know why you changed our plans. You've got enough money. What are another eight weeks going to do?"

"You just don't get it, do you?" Eisler said. "That kid's bringing in millions. We could keep this thing going for another year and drag a fortune out of it."

"You've already dragged a fortune out. Don't be greedy."

"You might be right. Sol Lowy put a team of auditors into Shanghai to account for his containers. Our people up there got wind of it just in time. We replaced the plates on over five hundred containers and when the auditors checked they accounted for all Sol's serial numbers. Fools." Eisler laughed. "I was more worried that Sol would find out about Ocean Cargo Containers. Christ, if he knew we owned it, we'd be dead, but that's something no one will ever find out. It's funny, when Paul and I formed the company, it was almost honest."

"That must have been before my time."

"We were taking a buying commission upfront and taking a profit on the sale of the containers that clients didn't know about. We had a client with a million bucks who wanted two hundred and fifty containers, and we couldn't get the steel. It looked like we were going to lose the business when Paul came up with the idea of invoicing him and manufacturing after we got the steel. We raised an invoice, stuck some fake serial numbers on it, and voila we had a million bucks in the bank and hadn't supplied anything."

"You never did manufacture them."

"It was so easy, we just kept on doing it," Eisler said. "We raised invoices for fifty thousand containers and manufactured about fifteen thousand. Some of the small-timers wanted to see their containers. We always had some new containers available, so we whacked plates with their serial numbers on them, and the fools were as happy as pigs in shit. Other than Sol and that nuisance Evert, we've never had a problem. As long as the suckers got their income checks every quarter, they were happy."

"Simon, why didn't you pay Evert? It was only three and a half million, and it would've kept him quiet?"

"I should've, but I knew if I could hold him off for a few more weeks, we'd be in Croatia living a life of luxury. It just seemed silly to pay him when I could stall. I got too greedy."

"Yes, you did, but you got lucky when that cop shot him. Can you imagine what he might have told the media?"

"It had nothing to do with luck."

"What? What do you mean?"

"Forget it. It was a slip of the tongue."

I felt the hair on the back of my neck stand up. I'd been right. Tobias Evert had been murdered. Eisler had somehow gotten the SFPD to do his dirty work. They weren't vigilantes, they were murderers.

Barbara paused, obviously taken aback, before saying, "Okay, Simon, as you wish. Do you want me to organize the airline bookings? I can't wait to be on that beautiful island."

"Hell, no. It's far too early. Look, Barbara, you'd better get going. Paul will be here soon."

After Barbara left, I heard Eisler sit down at the coffee table and pour himself a drink. I guess he was waiting for Wiese. Ten minutes later, he switched off the lights and left. There was no sign of Paul Wiese, and Eisler hadn't called him. What was going on?

Chapter 22

I WAITED FOR A few minutes before removing the painting and opening the safe. As I'd hoped, I was looking at a file marked Tobias Evert. It was thin, maybe forty pages, and there was another even thinner file below it. I didn't look inside them as I strode down to the photocopier outside my office. In less than five minutes, I was back in Eisler's office carefully putting the files back where I'd found them.

I was about to close the safe when I took out the travel agency folder. There were some brochures on Croatia inside it, Eisler's passport, and one first-class ticket for him, one-way on American Airlines to Hong Kong. I was confused. The travel date was in a week's time, not eight weeks. It wasn't to Croatia, but Hong Kong and it was a one way ticket. Where was Barbara's ticket? Was Wiese going to be traveling independently? I copied the contents, put the folder back in the safe and closed it. I checked the office one more time and went back to the photocopier and did the same. When I was certain I'd left nothing behind, I left the offices with the copies of the documents tucked inside my pants, and hidden below my jacket. By the time I walked out onto California Street, I was fairly sure that Eisler was about to bail, and leave his partners in crime to face the music.

I got back to my apartment, dropped the papers on the kitchen table and made myself a strong, black coffee. I never drank black coffee. I'd heard guys in the forces swear that it helped them with their thinking. I was hoping it would do the same for me. Henry Nelson had explained to me what a Ponzi scheme was, but I hadn't suspected Eisler and Wiese were pulling the same scam with shipping containers. I googled Ponzi and refreshed myself on how these schemes worked. Bernie Madoff's name appeared frequently. No wonder, he had run the biggest Ponzi scheme ever, ripped off investors for billions, and been sentenced to one hundred and fifty years.

I hadn't known it when I was copying Mr. Evert's file, but six sheets were blank bar for his signature. He had put far too much trust in Eisler. There were invoices from Ocean Cargo Containers for nine hundred containers costing three and a half million dollars. God knows how many of them really existed, but probably no more than two hundred and fifty. There was a note about Evert mortgaging his house to borrow more than a million dollars from the bank and increasing the limit on his credit card to one hundred thousand. Strangely Evert had authorized Summit to convert his quarterly income into more containers. I say strangely because, without that income, he could not meet the interest payments on his loan or make credit card payments. I looked at the authority and compared it to one of the signed blank sheets. The signature on the authority was in the identical position to that on the blank sheet. Barbara Sumner had witnessed the signature on the authority. It seemed obvious to me that someone had typed the authority above the signature on a blank sheet, but, if that were the case, why hadn't Evert complained or gone to the authorities when he didn't receive any income? There were several phone messages from

Barbara Sumner to Eisler about Evert calling and wanting a million dollars of his money back. Eisler had scrawled on one.

This is nothing to worry about. His wife doesn't know about the mortgage. He won't take any legal action.

I knew that Mrs. Evert was almost certain to lose her house unless she could extract some cash from Summit.

The documents I'd copied from the second file were bank statements in the names of Chinese companies in Shanghai, Hong Kong, Liechtenstein, the Caymans and Ireland. I did a quick conversion and added them up. They aggregated more than fifty million dollars, and I had no doubt it was cash that Eisler, Wiese, and Sumner had ripped off from investors.

I had learned a lot, but I didn't know what I could do about it. If I informed the authorities, they'd shut the business down and throw Eisler and his partners in jail. That wouldn't help Mrs. Evert one bit because the authorities might never recover the monies from the international banks. Even if they did, she would probably only get a few cents on the dollar, and by the time she did, the mortgagee would most likely have already foreclosed.

I was also distressed that I was being used to fleece new investors and had no doubt that I'd feel their wrath after Summit was exposed. When I thought about this, I felt sick.

It was 2:00 a.m. when I got to bed, and I spent the night tossing and turning. I couldn't stop thinking about Georgie and her mother, knowing there was nothing I could do to help them. When I wasn't thinking about Georgie, I was thinking about my own sleazy role at Summit. Just after 4:00 a.m., a ridiculous idea came to me. Five minutes later, I was on my laptop checking flights, rental cars, and accommodation.

Chapter 23

WHEN I EVENTUALLY WOKE up, I was tired but excited. I called Georgie, and we agreed to meet for lunch at the Sausalito Bakery & Café which was close to her home. When I got out of the cab, I saw her sitting under an umbrella at a table at the front of the café. She got up as I approached and kissed me on both cheeks. "How was last night?" she asked.

I told her what I had done, not leaving anything out, other than that I was almost certain her father had been murdered. That would have to wait for a more appropriate time and place.

"My God," she said, "what would have you done if they'd seen you?"

"I don't know."

"I knew you were lying about drinks. Why didn't you tell me? I could've kept watch at the front of the building."

I laughed. "I wouldn't want you standing on a dark street for two hours. Besides, I work better alone."

"Explain to me again what a Ponzi scheme is?"

"Think of it this way," I said. "Ten investors each make a ten-thousand-dollar investment in a fund. At the end of the first month, the fund pays them each two hundred dollars in income. The two hundred paid out is the investor's own money, but he thinks he's earning twenty-four percent per annum. The investors are happy, so they tell their friends about their great investment, and they invest as well. The fund pays the friends the same rate, and they tell their friends, and so the cycle continues. As long as there are new investors, it can go on forever, but it never does."

"Why not?"

"There'll be a time when some of the investors want their money back and won't be able to get it, or it will take too long. Word will leak out, and there'll be a run on the fund, and it won't be able to pay. The promoters will be exposed, but the savvy cons don't let that happen. While the money is still pouring in, they build up a nest egg of investors' funds and then just disappear overnight." I grimaced.

"Like Eisler's going to do," Georgie said.

"Exactly."

"We have to go to the police."

"If we do your mother will lose her house. We can't," I said, not wanting to say I didn't know if there were anyone in the SFPD with any power who we could trust. I'd trust Rafter and Enright, but I had the impression those with more power in the force might bury them.

"She's going to lose it anyway."

"Maybe not. I have a plan." I smiled. "Do you feel like eating?"

"I couldn't. I'll just have coffee."

Without asking her, I ordered two strong, short blacks. I thought we'd need them. Then I explained my plan. I finished by saying, "It's a long shot, but greed is all we've got. Let's pray Eisler takes the bait. It's lucky you're a web designer."

"And you said you weren't smart." Finally, there was a smile on Georgie's face, and she squeezed my hand. "I'm going with you. Hadn't you better call him and make sure he'll see us?"

Ernie Post answered on the second ring, and if he were surprised to hear from me, he sure didn't show it. "Howdy, Chad. We've been hearin' alls about you," he said. "What do you want tuh see me about?"

I knew there was no point correcting him on my name. "Ernie, I need you to do me a favor," I said, and then hurriedly added. "I'm coming to Floydada, and I need to see you. It won't cost you anything."

"Floydada, huh? You used to call it home. How long will you be stayin'?"

"We'll be flying in on Monday and leaving first thing on Tuesday. We're coming specially to see you."

"We?" he asked.

"I'll have a good friend with me. You'll really like her." I could almost hear his brain turning over and knew he was mulling over what he'd just heard.

"What time will you be here?" He finally asked.

"We land at Lubbock at 1:30 p.m. and expect to be at your store within the hour."

"I'll see you then," he said, and I heard the dial tone.

I put my cell on the table and looked at Georgie who had a huge smirk on her face. "I'm a 'good friend', am I?"

I felt myself going red.

"I'm sorry," she said, giving me a playful push in the chest. "You're not the typical male, are you?"

I ignored her question. "I better arrange the flights and rent a car."

"I'll pay. After all, you're only doing this because of mom and me."

I wouldn't hear of it, but the accommodation was a real

problem. I would've stayed in the cheapest digs I could find, but now I had to find somewhere half-decent. I opted for the La Quinta Inn in Lubbock which looked presentable, was less than a hundred bucks, and was close to the airport. I then wrestled with a bigger problem. Did I book two rooms or one? It had nothing to do with the money. I just didn't want to look like a fool.

On Sunday night, I called Paul Wiese and told him something urgent had come up. I had to go to Floydada and wouldn't be in the office until Wednesday. He wasn't happy and muttered something about big new clients who were expecting to meet me. I didn't care; I was just glad I wouldn't play any part in fleecing them.

Chapter 24

UA 1246 TO LUBBOCK via Denver departed on time at 6:45 a.m. Georgie held my hand on takeoff. I'd never been more relaxed with a woman. We chatted and refined our plans about how we were going to handle Ernie Post. I'd lost a little confidence and thought the chances of my hair-brained scheme succeeding were remote. Georgie had no such reservations and told me, "It's going to lift such a burden off mom when she gets her money back."

What expectations had I created? This was a long shot, and the odds were stacked against us.

We landed right on schedule at Lubbock, and threw our bags into the Chevy Spark that I'd rented for the fifty-mile drive to Floydada. An hour later I pulled up at the front of Ernie's Fishing and Recreation. It was a large timber corner store with double doors, and the front windows were crammed with fishing rods, reels, tents, outdoor gear, and boots. We walked inside, and like the windows, the store seemed massively overstocked. One wall was dedicated to rifles that were packed inside a long, glass cabinet. The once dark wood floor had faded and was covered with a layer of dust.

Ernie came from behind the counter and warmly welcomed me. "It's good tuh see you, Chad," he said, his calloused hand crushing mine.

"You too, Ernie. I'd like you to meet Georgie Evert."

"Uh huh, the good friend." He grinned, stroking his untidy gray beard. "It's a pleasure."

I looked around and said, "I don't think this place has changed in twenty years."

"Why would I want tuh change anythang? I like it, my customers like it, and my employees like it. Don't you, boys," he said, looking at two young men wearing jackets with Ernie's Fishing and Recreation embossed on the pockets. "Take care of the store. I'll be in my office."

We followed Ernie out to his office. It was large, dusty and cluttered. He nodded to two old fabric chairs, and we sat down. The heads of moose, boar, and coyote looked down from the walls at us. Directly behind his desk in pride of place was the head of a cougar. "Can I get you coffee or tea?"

"No, thanks. We were looked after on the plane," I replied.

"Okay, you've had a very long trip. Why don't you tell me why you needed tuh see me so urgently?"

I explained everything that had occurred from the time Mr. Evert had been killed.

"That's terrible. I feel so sorry for you, Miss," Ernie said, patting Georgie's arm, "but, Chad, I don't see how I can help."

"Do you remember about a year ago someone with a Floydada address won a thirteen million dollar share of the lottery?" I asked.

"Sure. A lot of folks thought it was old Jed Barrow, but it wasn't. He ain't got nothin'. No one knows who it is. Whoever it is, is playin' his cards close tuh his chest. What's that got tuh do with the scam?"

"I'd like you to pose over the phone as my uncle, Tom Denton, the winner of the thirteen million."

"Are you mad?" Ernie growled. "Yer uncle never won the lottery. He's a hermit. He lives off the land, and we never see him in town. Besides, he's tuh mean tuh have even bought a lottery ticket."

"Let me throw some light on it," I said and then went over my plan.

"I like it." Ernie grinned. "I'd like tuh help yer mama get her money back, Miss, and I'll do anythang I can tuh make sure she does."

"Thank you, Ernie." Georgie smiled. "You're very kind. Who do you bank with, and may we have one of your old statements?"

"PlainsCapital Bank, and why do you want one of my statements?" Ernie asked, his face clouded in doubt.

I filled Ernie in and added, "Can you log onto your account and let us have a print copy of the screen?"

"Yeah, yeah. Yer fixin' tuh scam the scammers. I like it. I really like it," Ernie said. Then he paused. "Hey, I can't get intuh any trouble with the law for this, can I?"

"Ernie, nothing that you're going to do is against the law, and no one will be able to trace anything to you. Everything will be in the name of Tom Denton." I reached for my wallet and took out a hundred-dollar bill. "Here. This will cover the cost of the burner phone."

"I don't want yer money," Ernie said, pushing my hand away. "This'll be a real pleasure."

"Thanks, Ernie." I grinned, patting him on the back.

It was after 5:30 p.m., and Ernie had been glancing at his watch for fifteen minutes. "I wish I could take you tuh supper," he said, "but I've got a Chamber of Commerce meetin', and I can't miss it. I'm sorry. Chad, a lot of folks think you ran out on the town. Thought you were tuh good for it. I know it's baloney, but you should watch your step. There are some hotheads who'd like tuh brang you down a peg or two."

We thanked him and left.

"Are we going to eat here?" Georgie asked.

"There's not much in the way of restaurants," I said. "Let's eat in Lubbock."

"Are you worried about what Ernie said?"

"No, I'm not. It's just that this was Chad Denton's hometown, and he's long dead and buried. Josh Kennelly has no affinity with it. Besides, the eateries in Lubbock are far better. We'll go to the motel, get cleaned up, and then find a nice restaurant."

The La Quinta Inn was pretty much as depicted on its website. A two-level cream-colored motel that was clean and well presented. The check-in area was tiled, and we faced a long wooden counter as we walked in. I handed over my credit card, and the woman behind the counter handed me the keys and told us how to find our rooms. As we walked out into the night air, I heard Georgie giggling. "What's funny?" I asked.

"I wondered whether you'd get one or two rooms. You're really sweet."

I had no idea what to say. Georgie put her arm around my shoulders, something no other woman had ever done and started giggling again. "I would've been happy sharing. I know I can trust you."

"I wasn't sure," I muttered.

"You should have asked."

We looked up restaurants in Lubbock on Urbanspoon and found that the 'Italian Gardens' was nearby, and was ranked fourth out of over five hundred restaurants in Lubbock. It turned out to be a small, cozy, family-owned restaurant, and the food was sensational. While we were waiting for our veal parmesan, we nibbled on stuffed mushroom appetizers. After we'd finished our main course, we noticed the couple at the table next to us eating chocolate cannoli, and the temptation was too much. Georgie was bubbling and telling me what a relief it would be for her mother when she got her money back and paid the bank. She was talking as if it was a fait accompli which really worried me. So much had to go right, but I just smiled and nodded, reluctant to spoil her mood. We strolled back to the motel, arms linked and happy with what we'd achieved.

"Come into my room," Georgie said, "I want to show you something." She flicked on her laptop. "What do you think?"

I was looking at the home page of the PlainsCapital Bank. "I'm sorry, I don't understand," I said, scratching my head.

"It's not the bank's website. It's my creation. Do you think it'll fool your bosses?"

"My God, it fooled me. It's identical. It's brilliant. When did you get the time to do it?"

"While I was waiting for you to shower and make yourself beautiful." She giggled, got out of her chair, and put her arms around my neck. Then she started kissing me, and I pulled her toward me until we were locked together. My hormones were running wild. "We have to get up early in the morning, Josh. What a shame."

"Yeah," I said, as I felt her arms release from my waist.

As I opened the door, she gave me a mischievous smile and said, "Am I still a good friend?"

Chapter 25

WE LANDED IN SAN FRANCISCO just after 1:30 p.m. and took a cab to the Westfield Center in Market Street. We needed an off-white paper that was the same or similar to what the Plains Capital Bank used for customers' statements. Maido Stationery & Gifts was the most likely place we'd find it. We didn't expect a perfect match, but what we found was similar in texture and color. We paid the shop assistant and were about to leave, when I said, "Do you have a letter template and fine black pens? I want something that's permanent and can't be erased."

"We have just what you're looking for. It can be hidden with white ink or tape though."

I grinned. "I'm not worried about that. Let me have the template and two pens."

"What was that about?" Georgie asked.

"I'll tell you later," I said.

We had no time to waste and were soon in another cab on the way to Sausalito. I'd done some calculations for interest and bank fees on the plane and had prepared handwritten calculations of what Tom Denton's bank statements would look like. Now it was up to Georgie to weave her magic and produce a PlainsCapital bank statement in the name of my uncle, Tom Denton, that would pass for the real thing. She turned her computer and printer on before making me a sandwich and a cup of coffee. "Here," she said, handing them to me. "Why don't you go in the living room, put your feet up, and watch some television?"

"You don't want my help?"

"I need to concentrate. I've got Ernie's bank statement and your calculations. Sorry. There's nothing more you can do."

I must have dozed off. Georgie gently shook me. "Wake up, sleepy head. You've been out for nearly two hours." She laughed. "Come and see what I've done."

I followed her into the spare bedroom where she'd set her computer on a small card table. There were two PlainsCapital bank statements next to the printer, and Georgie passed them to me. "What do you think?"

They were nearly perfect. She had trimmed the paper with a paper cutter, and it was identical in size to Ernie's bank statement. The red and black colors used on Tom Denton's fake statements were identical to the real thing. Only the off-white color of the statement was slightly different. "They're brilliant. No one's going to doubt their authenticity. God, you're good."

"I thought you'd like them." She smiled. Her teeth were as white as snow, and she had full, inviting lips. She was just so wholesome and sexy. I kicked myself. My thoughts had strayed, but I refocused knowing time was running out.

"Let me have a two-hole punch and a couple of different colored pens," I said, "and can you get my coffee cup?"

I punched holes in each of the statements separately, so they didn't align. Then I put ticks over one in blue and the other in red. Georgie handed me my cup, and I splashed the dregs over one of the pages as if it had spilled.

"Very clever," she said, as she opened the fake PlainsCapital website and went to the page marked accounts. A box appeared showing a variety of banking services and asked for a username and password. Georgie chose online banking and typed in the username and password she'd created. Tom Denton's account appeared with identical transactions to that on the statements.

"Perfect," I said.

"The best is yet to come." She laughed. "Watch this." She hit the tab marked transfers, and a box appeared with the top section showing the balance of the account – $13,520,107.46. Below it, were blank sections for the transferee's name, bank number, account number, and the amount, along with details of the transfer. The bottom section showed the balance after any transfer had been made.

"I don't remember that bottom section."

"I added it," she replied. "Eisler's going to want confirmation of the transfer to Summit's bank account which he's not going to get. However, I think if he sees the cash disappear from Tom Denton's account, it'll satisfy him. Watch this." She typed in some transfer details, the sum of six million dollars, and hit the button marked remit, and, voila, I was looking at a balance of $7,520,107.46.

"Fantastic! It's all done."

"Not quite. I'm going to add a few more pages. I'd hate it if you got fat fingers, hit the wrong tab, and nothing happened," she said, standing and stretching.

I put my hands on her hips and drew her toward me. We kissed, and she snuggled into me. I tried to stop my body from involuntarily thrusting. We were next to the bed, and, in one deft movement, I lifted her onto it. I was breathing heavily, and Georgie's face was flushed. God, she was so beautiful. We were locked together, and I pulled away ever so slightly and started to undo her blouse. She didn't resist. I unhooked her bra and fondled her firm breasts. She was all but naked from the waist up. I put my hand on the top button of her jeans and was about to undo it, when we heard the front door. Georgie pushed me away in one swift movement and buttoned her blouse.

"It's Mom." She giggled. "I'd better go and say hello."

"I'll come with you."

"No, you won't. Not in that condition," she said, staring at my pants. "Mom's not going to want to see that." She leaned over and kissed me. "I'll tell her you're working on the computer. Come out when you're decent."

Ten minutes later I sheepishly said hello to Mrs. Evert and apologized. I told her that I'd been in the middle of something that I had to finish. She insisted I join them for dinner, but I declined, telling her that I had to mentally prepare for tomorrow. Instead, I agreed to have a cup of coffee which was accompanied by a plate of freshly baked cupcakes. As I sipped my coffee, I could feel Georgie's eyes on me, and when I looked at her, she smiled impishly at me.

It was going to be a huge day tomorrow, and I apologized again to Mrs. Evert and said that I had to get home. We heard the cab beep and Georgie came out onto the front porch with me.

"You're driving me crazy," I said.

"It's mutual," she replied, kissing me. "Good luck."

Chapter 26

THE STREETLIGHTS WERE JUST coming on when the cab dropped me off at my apartment, and I immediately went out to buy fresh milk. While at the store, I picked up a copy of the *Chronicle*. There was an article on the third page that caught my attention. Hamish Gidley-Baird had been robbed, savagely beaten, and left for dead in a parking garage. The article went on to say that he was recuperating in The San Francisco Private Hospital and wasn't expected to return to work for at least two weeks. Two weeks! It must have been one hell of a beating. Police had no leads and said it was most likely the homeless making a quick score. I thought it was far more than that. The hospital was only about three miles away, and visiting hours were until 8:00 p.m. I wanted to talk to Hamish, and could be there in forty minutes if I walked briskly.

The hospital was quiet, obviously expensive, and patients had private rooms. The severe looking nurse on reception quizzed me, and when I told her I wasn't related to Hamish, she said, "Sorry, he's only seeing relatives. You'll have to come back when he's feeling better. Give him a few more days."

I was frustrated and said, "Look. It's important. Can you tell him it's Josh Kennelly and that I have to see him? I might be able to help him."

"Help? How can you help?" she scoffed, and then her face

softened. "I recognize you. You're the hero. The guy on the ledge of that building on California Street. That was you, wasn't it?"

"Yes, ma'am, that was me, but it was blown out of proportion."

"I don't think so," she said, picking up the phone. "Julie, can you check with Mr. Gidley-Baird and ask him if he's up to seeing a visitor, Mr. Josh Kennelly. If he's sleeping, don't disturb him."

A few minutes later the phone buzzed, and the nurse looked at me and said, "You're in luck. He'll see you. Take a seat. Julie will be here in a few minutes to take you to his room."

As I followed Julie down the corridor, I couldn't help contrasting the peacefulness with the pandemonium of the Jimmy Carter Memorial. The *Chronicle* was obviously looking after Hamish because his accommodation was more like a five-star hotel room than a hospital ward. He was propped up on pillows, and when I looked at him, I momentarily lost my breath. I'd seen a lot worse in the Middle East, but in civilian life, it was the worst I'd ever seen. His head was in bandages, but I could see his eyes. They were black and swollen. His nose was twisted, and his lips were huge. If it were the homeless, they would have stolen his wallet and run. Once they had the cash, there was no way they were going to hang around and beat the crap out of him. I was no expert, but common sense told me this was a hate crime.

He held one skinny arm up and grinned. He'd lost most of his front teeth. "Josh Kennelly," he said, "this is an honor. You're a bit of a blur because I can't get my glasses on."

There was a thick pair of bifocals sitting on the set of drawers next to him. "Jesus, they did a job on you," I said, as I took a chair next to the bed. From what I could see of his frame, a decent wind would blow him over.

"Wrong place, wrong time." He grimaced, obviously in pain. "What brings you here?"

"Who do you think did it?"

"The police say it was the homeless. They took my wallet, ring, watch, loose change, and overcoat. They were desperate."

"Do you believe that?"

"What are you getting at?"

"You're doing a series of articles exposing the SFPD and no doubt you've made some powerful enemies. Surely that crossed your mind?"

"Of course, but in two weeks I'll have recovered and still be writing those articles. Besides, if it were them, wouldn't they have warned me off when they were beating me? They never said a word," he said, letting out an involuntary whine.

"You're hurting. Would you prefer it if I came back another time?"

"I'm okay. What do you think?"

"You're thinking too logically," I said. "What if the motive was hate. What if someone in the SFPD got sick of reading your articles, stewed over them, and decided to beat the hell out of you just for pleasure? The stuff they stole could have been just for show."

"Is that what you think happened?"

"It's what my gut tells me. Who told you it was the homeless?"

"The police. They said it was obvious."

"Do they have any leads?"

"No," but they said, "my watch and the ring will eventually show up, and that's when they'll catch them."

His arms were bruised, and I could see he was uncomfortable. "Did they break your ribs too?"

"Three," he said, "and I've got severe bruising of the buttocks and legs. The police think they kept on kicking me after I lost consciousness. Said they were probably meth heads."

I had no doubt it was a hate crime. They'd beaten the poor bastard to a pulp, and it wasn't like he'd presented any physical threat. I didn't need to be a Rhodes Scholar to see that he was weak. "Do you mind if I have a word with the police who are handling it?"

"No," he said, "they left a card on top of the drawers."

I reached over and picked it up — Detective Matthew Lanza. "Detectives Lanza and Selwood." I scowled.

"Do you know them?"

"It's a long story. Tell me, did you get a look at your attackers?"

"The police asked me that, and I'll tell you what I told them. They were wearing hoodies, it was dark, and I didn't see anything."

"Are you sure. You must have gotten a glimpse of their faces."

"Yeah, but only enough to know that they were white."

"You told the police that?"

"Yes."

"If you saw their faces, you must have seen more. The shape of their noses, their lips, teeth, eye color, eyebrows, nose rings, anything."

He closed his eyes. I didn't know whether it was because he was concentrating or if I'd exhausted him and he was dozing. "You haven't answered my question. Why are you here?" he asked.

I explained the events that had occurred since Mr. Evert lost his life and the pressure Lanza and Selwood had applied to get me to tip a bucket on Lieutenant Rafter.

"Now I see. You think there's a connection to the articles I've been writing."

"I'm certain."

"Well, if they think I'm going to ease up, they're sadly mistaken," he said, sticking his chin out.

"Good. Now can you think back to that night and their faces? The slightest clue might help."

When he closed his eyes this time he had a pained expression, and I knew he was concentrating. "Sorry," he said.

I stood up. "Thanks for trying. I hope you're out of here soon."

As I reached the door, he said, "Wait. I know this is not much, but I just remembered, one of them had thick, bushy red eyebrows."

I grinned. "It wasn't the homeless who attacked you. Whatever you do, don't tell Lanza and Selwood. Be careful with anything you tell them. They're not on your side."

Chapter 27

I CALLED GEORGIE ON the way to the office and asked her to find out where Officer Carl Penske lived. I think she knew what I was up to and resisted. "I can't get that information," she said. "I can't access the police's database."

"I've seen you on a computer. I know what you can do."

"I can't," she repeated.

I didn't want to lie, but sometimes you have no choice. "I wouldn't be asking if it weren't vital in getting your mom's money back."

She paused before responding, "I want to help, but really, I don't have the skills to hack into databases. I'm a web designer, not a computer hacker. There might be another way though. Leave it with me."

When I reached the office, Mandy said that Paul Wiese was looking for me. I'd heard on the grapevine that Kirsty was out of the hospital but was so traumatized it would be months before she could return to work. I made a mental note to visit her at home.

I disregarded the message about Wiese and strode down to Simon Eisler's office and asked Barbara if he were free. "You're not the flavor of the month," she said. "What makes you think you can just disappear for two days? We've had some very unhappy clients who came in especially to meet you." While she was berating me, she picked up the intercom and asked Eisler if he would see me. A few minutes later I was sitting opposite him.

"Mr. Eisler," I said, pulling out my checkbook, "I want to make a twenty-thousand-dollar investment in shipping containers." It was eighty percent of my net worth, but I needed to establish my credibility. When Summit fell over, I wanted to appear as a naïve victim rather than a crook. It was a small price to pay.

Eisler yawned and shook his head. For all his interest, I might just as well have dropped a turd on his desk. "You don't need to see me. Sort it out with Paul. Oh, and what makes you think you can piss off on private business any time you like?"

It was the perfect opening. "It wasn't private," I said, "well, not totally. My uncle was one of the winners of the lottery about a year ago. He got thirteen million out of it, and it's been in the bank ever since earning a pittance. He saw me on television and called to say he wanted me to give him some investment advice. He wants to invest six million dollars in shipping containers."

The figurative turd must have turned to gold. Eisler beamed. "How?" he asked. "How did you get him interested?"

"I've been listening to Paul give his spiel to clients for a week. I could repeat it word for word in my sleep," I said. "It was easy."

"When's he going to make the investment?"

"He wants to do it quickly and was going to see his accountant first thing this morning."

"Are you sure he's not leading you on? Some of these good ol' boys are full of shit."

I opened my satchel and passed him the two bank statements.

"Holy fuck," he exclaimed, "he's been earning nothing. The bank's been screwing him."

I passed Eisler another document.

"What's this?" he asked, barely looking at it.

It was headed, Thomas Denton, Client Profile in large letters but Eisler paid it no heed.

"It's my uncle's investment profile. You can see that preservation of capital is his primary goal. He's a conservative investor. It is a safe investment, isn't it?"

"Yeah, of course, as safe as the Bank of England. When do we see his money?"

"Hopefully, today," I said. As if on cue, Barbara's voice came over the intercom saying, "Josh, it's Mr. Denton, he says he has to speak to you."

"Tell him I'll call him back in ten minutes."

I thought Eisler was going to have a heart attack. "Don't tell him that. Go and talk to him. Don't lose him. Jeez, Josh, what are you doing?"

"He's fine," I said. "I know Paul's got a lot of appointments lined up and, as you've just seen, my uncle can be very demanding."

"Forget Paul. He can take care of his own appointments. You don't need to be there. Listen to me, your uncle's number one priority, and until you've got him tucked away, I don't want you working on anything else. Now, for Chrissake, go and call him."

I didn't move.

"What's wrong?" Eisler asked. "Why are you still sitting there?"

"How much do I get out of this deal?"

Eisler smirked, and I heard him mutter, "When you strip away the skin, we're all the same. How does a hundred thousand sound?"

"I thought it'd be more," I replied. No matter what figure he'd said, that was going to be my answer. "I'm going to use it to buy more containers."

"Who said greed's not good?" Eisler laughed. "Get the deal done this week, and I'll pay you one-twenty. Now get out of here and call your uncle."

I picked up the bank statements and profile and went back to my office. Eisler was on the hook, but it wasn't going to be easy to reel him in.

Eisler buzzed me three times during the morning for progress reports, and when I looked up from my desk just after midday, he was standing at my door.

"What's happening? "What did his accountant say? Why haven't you closed the deal?"

I hung my head. "I'm sorry. We have a problem. Did you know that Tobias Evert had a daughter?"

"Yes, of course. What's she got to do with your uncle?"

"Well, she was on community radio yesterday saying we owed her mother over three and a half million dollars and wouldn't pay. My uncle's accountant heard her and told my uncle about it. Now he wants to talk to her. His accountant said she's getting interviewed on a mainstream radio station tomorrow. Shit!"

Eisler was unruffled. "Don't worry, Josh. This is just a hiccup. Get your uncle on speakerphone and let's talk to him."

I punched in Ernie's number and said a silent prayer. "Uncle Tom," I said, "it's me again. You're on speakerphone. I'm with my boss, Mr. Eisler, he's the financial genius I told you about."

"Have you got that girl's name and phone number 'cause yer wastin' yer time if you haven't?" Ernie responded.

"I told you, you don't need to talk to her. This is a terrific investment, and you're gonna be kicking yourself if you pass on it," I said.

Eisler looked at me and put a finger to his lips. "Tom," he said. "Can I call you Tom? It's Simon Eisler. I've been looking over your file with your nephew. Your bank hasn't done you any favors."

"Call me what you like, sonny, and yeah, I know the bank hasn't been payin' much, but my money's safe," Ernie said.

"I understand," Eisler replied, "but our investments are safe too, and with us, you get a decent return. I can't think of anything much safer than steel shipping containers. Can you?"

"Yeah, they're appealin' all right, and that's why I'm lookin' at 'em. My accountant heard the daughter of the guy who got shot sayin' that y'all wouldn't pay her mother the money you owed her. What have you got tuh say about that?"

"Tom, it's not our liability. It's the container company's, and they've never failed to make a payment since we've been dealing with them. However, they need twenty-one days' notice, so they can place the containers with other investors. That's not unreasonable, is it?"

"It's more than twenty-one days since that guy got killed, and the family still doesn't have its money," Ernie said. There was a long pause, but we could hear him breathing. "Chad, you said that I'd only be dealin' with you, and now I find that when I want tuh realize my investment, I'll be dealin' with some mob in China I've never heard of. I'm startin' tuh not like the sound of this deal."

"Uncle Tom, your investment will be as safe as houses," I yelled. "Your accountant's confusing you. Don't listen to him. Listen to me!"

Eisler was looking at me shaking his head furiously and crossing and uncrossing his arms in front of him. "Tom, you're right. We've completely overhauled the structure we had with the Chinese, and our clients now deal with us on all matters. You'll be talking to and being advised by Josh exclusively," Eisler said. "You have nothing to worry about."

"Who's Josh?" Ernie responded.

"Chad," I whispered to Eisler.

"Sorry, Tom, a slip of the tongue. I meant Chad. Can I put you down for fifteen hundred containers? We can put them to work straight away."

There was another long pause. "You sound like a real straight shooter, Simon, but I want tuh talk tuh that girl. I'm sorry, that's the way it is."

I was about to say something when Eisler actually put his hand over my mouth and said, "I'll see what I can do, Tom. If that's what it's going to take to satisfy you, we'll do it. With us, the client's always right."

"Thanks, I guess I'll be hearin' from you," Ernie said, and we heard the dial tone.

Eisler glared at me. "Jeez, Josh, you can't talk to clients like that. You can't lose your temper. You have to sweet talk them, at least until you've got their money. Do you think you can handle this deal? Do you want me to take over dealing with your uncle?"

My ploy had worked. "Mr. Eisler, I might have lost it for a while, but my uncle will only deal with me. Sorry, it won't happen again."

"For Chrissake, call me Simon," Eisler said, leaving my office.

Two minutes later he was back. He was frowning. "Josh, you

couldn't have cared less when I doubled and then trebled your salary. Why the change?"

I laughed. "There's a big difference. The raise is spread over a year, whereas the hundred and twenty grand is for a day's work."

"You're not wrong, even though it looks like it might be two days," Eisler replied. "Thanks, you've restored my lack of faith in human nature."

Chapter 28

EISLER BUZZED ME AGAIN at 2:30 p.m., and I told him I'd spoken to my uncle three more times but was getting nowhere. He summoned me to his office, and I called Ernie on the speakerphone and Eisler really poured it on about honesty and integrity.

"Surely, you can trust your own nephew, Tom," he said.

"I ain't seen him for ten years, and then I call him for a bit of advice and next thang you know he's on my doorstep trying tuh hustle me. I tell–"

"Hustle you? I never tried to hustle you," I shouted. "You asked, and I provided the best advice you're ever likely to get. Where the bloody hell do you get off calling me a hustler?"

Eisler's hands were working overtime as he tried to pacify me.

"How many times have you called me this afternoon? Six times? Eight times? Jeez, Chad, I don't hear from you for ages, and now y'all over me like a bad smell. I asked you for one thang. Tuh talk tuh the girl and all you've done is make excuses all day. What am I meant tuh think?"

I was about to let loose, but Eisler was shaking his head.

"Tom, her name is Georgina Evert," Eisler said, "I've got my PA trying to find her. I was shocked when you told me what your accountant had heard her say. I don't want people saying

135

bad things about our business. I don't know what her problem is, but trust me, I'm going to sort it out. I'm more than happy for you to talk to her."

"That's all I'm askin', Simon. Thanks for yer help. I guess you can tell my nephew ain't got no patience. It's nice tuh talk tuh someone with a bit of poise and experience. Chad, Rome wasn't built in a day."

We heard the phone clunk, and Eisler said, "I'm going to call Miss Evert and see if I can talk some sense into her."

"How'd you find her?" I asked.

"We had her details on her father's file. Barbara called her mom to get her daughter's phone number and found that she's staying with her. That was a bonus."

"She's bad mouthing us though. How's it going to help?"

"Listen and learn," Eisler said, punching a number into his handset. He didn't put it on speaker.

I braced myself. My plan was working, but it was dependent on how convincing Georgie was, and I hoped she was up to it. I sat and listened.

"Miss Evert, it's Simon Eisler. I run Summit Investments. I believe you're having some problems. I'm calling to see if I can help."

After a pause, he said, "Lawyers? No, I haven't seen any letters from your mother's lawyers. Why would she need lawyers?"

"Well, it's not our liability. Ocean Cargo Containers is the responsible party. I'm sure that payment is on the way."

Another pause. "Yes, I know it's more than twenty-one days. It's a large, financially strong company so you have nothing to worry about. Your mother's money is safe. Trust me."

Eisler didn't speak for more than two minutes, and I knew Georgie was making her pitch. Eisler's face was red, but when he spoke, he was perfectly calm.

"Yes, I know your father only dealt with Summit and me, but the guarantee is from Ocean Cargo Containers. Miss Evert, what you're asking is totally unreasonable. Yes, I know I said your mother's money is safe, but the liability isn't ours. Let me get this straight. You want us to make payment to your mother on behalf of Ocean Cargo Containers and then to recover the monies from them."

As I listened to Eisler, I felt like cheering. Georgie was obviously handling her part perfectly.

I watched Eisler clench and unclench his hands before saying, "You don't care whether we recover the monies or not. You just want what you consider is owed to your mother. Miss Evert, that's very harsh, particularly when there's no legal liability for us to pay."

Eisler's face was red, and his lips were compressed. Despite his apparent anger, he continued to maintain his composure and said, "Yes, yes, I appreciate that you're not cognizant of the legalities and that you're just trying to help your mother. Listen, I'm going to contact Ocean Cargo Containers just as soon as I finish this call. I'll see if I can get your mother's money."

There was another pause. "Yes, I'll see if I can get it transferred by tomorrow."

"That's nice, Miss Evert, but don't thank me yet. Your father always trusted me."

"Well, that's nice to know. I'm glad I've restored your confidence in the firm. Yes, I'll call you first thing in the morning."

When Eisler put the phone down his face was drawn, and clearly, the call had not gone as he'd expected. "Barbara," he shouted, "get Paul in here pronto." Then he looked at me and said, "I don't need you. You can go back to your office but don't phone your uncle. You've done enough damage on that front already."

It was late afternoon when I left the office. I called Georgie and said I'd meet her at the Sausalito Bakery & Café.

It was cold, and she was sitting at an inside table. We kissed and had a quick cuddle. I could tell by her face that she was bubbling and dying to tell me something. I ordered hot chocolates, and Georgie said, "Eisler called me about fifteen minutes ago. I think he's going to pay mom. He wants us to go to the office at ten o'clock in the morning. He said that mom has to sign some papers assigning her rights against Ocean Cargo Containers to Summit before he could make payment."

"What a load of rubbish. He's going to skip town on Friday night, and here he is getting sham paperwork executed. What a fraud he is. He can't help himself."

"I think your plan's going to work. Eisler said that if everything stacked up, he'd authorize the transfer while we're there. I told him I wouldn't be satisfied until our bank called to confirm the transfer. He said that we'd have confirmation by midday. You did it. You did it!" She laughed, jumping out of her chair and throwing her arms around my neck. "I love you."

As soon as the words slipped out, she turned red. She looked so vulnerable and gorgeous. "I've loved you since the minute I set eyes on you," I said, and felt her relax.

"That wasn't meant to come out, but I'm glad it did." Georgie smiled. "I was worried you might not feel the same."

"As if," I said. "Oh, I nearly forgot. Did you find out where Penske lives?"

"Yes, but before I tell you, I want to know why it's so important."

I told her what I had heard Eisler say that night about her father's killing having nothing to do with luck. She looked shocked and disappointed.

"I can't believe you didn't tell me."

"It sounded like it might have been a throwaway comment. It's the type of thing that men say when they're big-noting and trying to impress women with their cleverness."

"You don't believe it?"

"I don't know. I didn't tell you because I didn't want you running to the media or politicians and kicking up a fuss. If you had, there'd be no chance of getting your mother's money."

"I see," Georgie said, but I could see she didn't. "Why do you need Penske's address?"

I told her about Lanza and Selwood and what had happened at my apartment. "I think they might be part of a cover-up," I said. "They're protecting Penske, and it could be that they're just trying to help a fellow cop who was too anxious when he pulled the trigger. Worse, he could be a murderer, and they know it."

"God, why didn't you tell me?"

"I'm a loner when it comes to problem-solving, and I didn't want to see you get hurt if things went awry."

"Hmmm," she said, her frown dissipating. "I know you want to look after me, but if we're going to have a relationship, there can't be any secrets. What else haven't you told me?"

I told her about Hamish Gidley-Baird, explaining that I had

only found about his assault and robbery the prior night and had visited him in the hospital.

"Why do you want Penske's address?"

"I want to ask him some questions," I responded truthfully. "I think you can see why I didn't want to go to 3rd Street to do it."

"Here," she said, passing me a piece of paper.

"Jesus! A condo in Pacific Heights. How can he afford to live there on a cop's pay?"

"I thought the same. I checked it out on Google. It's opposite Lafayette Park in Gough Street – one bedroom with street parking."

"It's still a million bucks. How did you get his address?"

"I called and said that I was Kirsty's mom and that I wanted to express my gratitude to the fine, young policeman who saved her life. He wasn't in, but I gushed on and on about how wonderful he was, and that I'd baked a special cake for him and wanted to get it delivered to his home. Whoever I was talking to didn't want to tell me, but I just kept on rambling. In the end, I guess he thought the only way he could get rid of me was by giving me the address."

I gritted my teeth, and said, "That was risky. It was a long call, and they'll be able to trace the number to you if something untoward happens."

"Something untoward," she said, her eyes twinkling. "You have such a way with words. You said you were just going to ask him some questions, so what could go untoward?"

"Nothing, I suppose."

"Well, just in case something does, I used a burner phone, so the police aren't going to be able to trace me. You're not the only devious one, you know."

I burst out laughing. "Well done! We better get going."

On the way to Georgie's home we could see lights flickering from the boats on the bay. I had my arm tightly around her waist, and we couldn't have been closer. We stopped at the front of her house and started fondling. I'd never wanted someone more in my life. After ten minutes, we were groaning and breathing heavily. Georgie gently pushed me away and tidied herself up. "We better go inside. Mom will be getting worried."

"I'll just say hello," I said, "I have to prepare for tomorrow too."

Georgie's mother was more excited than her daughter, and I warned her to let Georgie do the talking in the morning. One slip and our little reverse scam would be blown wide apart. I didn't stay late. They were both overly exuberant, and I sensed they were going to have trouble sleeping.

Chapter 29

I AWOKE FROM A restless night's sleep, nervous and on edge. This was a new emotion for me. My nerves were all about Mrs. Evert and what we were going to try and pull off today. I crossed my fingers hoping she wouldn't make a mess of things. To be honest, when I dreamed up my plan, I thought the probability of it being successful was almost zero. Now, with a little luck and Georgie's acting skills, we just might pull it off.

I'd been in the office for nearly an hour when Barbara summoned me to Eisler's office for a meeting. I was surprised because I hadn't expected I'd be attending. I walked past Georgie and her mother sitting in the waiting area adjacent to Barbara's office. Georgie was wearing a black suit and had pulled her hair up in a bun in a failed attempt to make herself look severe.

"What's this about, Barbara?" I asked.

Before she could answer, Georgie stood up and said, "You're Mr. Kennelly, aren't you? I saw you on television. You tried to save my father, didn't you? I'm sorry we haven't thanked you before this. We've had so much on our minds."

This wasn't part of the script, but I immediately knew why Georgie had done it. "It was nothing," I murmured looking at my feet. "I'm sorry for your loss."

"Thank you," Georgie said, sitting back down.

Barbara tapped me on the shoulder, and whispered, "Josh, Mr. Eisler wants you to attend the meeting he's having with them. He said to tell you that you're not to say anything or get involved until he asks you something. He doesn't want you messing things up again."

"Okay, I've got the message," I whispered back. I knew exactly what Eisler was going to do. I thought he would've been a little more patient. I went into his office, and he directed me to take a chair at the boardroom table.

"I heard Miss Evert just thank you," he said. Don't think that means you can say anything. Keep your mouth shut unless I ask you a question. Understand?"

I nodded as Barbara showed Georgie and her mother into Eisler's office. "I'm Simon Eisler, and you've met Josh Kennelly," he said, before asking if they'd like anything to drink. They declined, and he got straight down to business.

"Mrs. Evert," Eisler said, "I'm sorry about your husband. His passing was so tragic for all of us. I must also apologize for this mix-up. I never even knew about your problems until your daughter explained them to me. It wasn't us. It was Ocean Cargo Containers. Somehow the paperwork got lost in Shanghai, but we've managed to track it down. If I can just get you to sign a few documents, we can sort this out and make a transfer into your bank account by no later than Monday."

"Thank you," Mrs. Evert replied, "that sounds fair."

I coughed and spluttered as if I had something stuck in my throat. Eisler glared at me. I apologized and excused myself to get a glass of water. I need not have worried. When I got back Georgie was saying, "Mr. Eisler, my mother doesn't understand financial transactions and, while I appreciate that your firm is not legally responsible, my father only ever dealt with you, and I hold you morally responsible. Your associate company has exceeded the twenty-one-day notice period, and yet you now expect us to wait even longer. We want our money today."

"That's very unfair," Eisler said, "and you realize that, even if you commenced legal action against Ocean Cargo Containers today, you still wouldn't have your money by Monday. I'm trying to help you."

"I appreciate your help. I really do. I realize the wheels of the law grind slowly, but I'm not talking about legal action. I'm being interviewed by Beverley Wiltshire on KQED this afternoon. I intend to tell her that you and Summit did not live up to the undertakings you made to my father. You might like to listen?" Georgie frowned.

"There's no point in trying to blackmail us," I said. "We're trying to do everything we can to help you."

Eisler glared at me but didn't say anything. "Miss Evert," he said, "if I can get your money today, are you still going to go ahead with the radio interview?"

"Why would I?" Georgie smiled.

Eisler tilted his chair and leaned back, pushing his hands through his hair. "What would your attitude to the firm be?"

"I don't understand?" Georgie replied.

"I would hate for you to speak ill of the firm," Eisler said.

"Speak ill? We would be eternally grateful," Georgie gushed. "We know that you have no legal obligation to pay us. It's just that we know that you have a lot more influence with Ocean Cargo Containers than we do. The minute I get confirmation from the bank that the funds have been deposited, I'll cancel the radio interview."

"Josh," Eisler said, "please witness Mrs. Evert's signature on these assignment documents." Then he turned to Georgie. "Miss Evert, we really shouldn't be doing this. We should only be making payment to the executors of your father's estate."

We had anticipated this. Georgie pulled a file from her satchel and handed Eisler two documents. "This is a notarized copy of my father's Will for your records. You'll see that my mother and I are the executors. The other document sets out details of the estate's bank account."

Eisler barked into the intercom, and Barbara appeared in an instant. He handed her the Will and bank details, telling her to immediately organize an electronic transfer of the amount due to the late Mr. Evert.

Then he said, "Josh, why don't you take the ladies out for coffee? I'll make sure there are no problems with the transfer. Miss Evert, you should have confirmation within the hour from your bank. I'd appreciate it if you could come back and let me know that everything's as you expected."

"Certainly," Georgie said.

Chapter 30

THE ELEVATOR WAS CROWDED, and we didn't speak, but I could see Georgie was bursting.

As we walked out onto California Street, I told Georgie and her mom not to show any emotion or familiarity. I'd hate to blow everything we'd achieved on the off chance that a zealous Summit employee saw us kissing and hugging, and reported it to Eisler. Consequently, our conversation while sipping coffee was subdued, but Georgie rubbed my leg with her foot under the table. It was obvious to me that she was bubbling, but I was determined to keep a somber composure. As I was ordering a second round of caffeine, Georgie's cell phone rang, and I heard her say, "The funds are in the account?" and then she paused before asking, "Are they cleared funds?"

She put the cell phone back in her handbag and looked at me. "The funds have been deposited, Mr. Kennelly. We should go back to your office so we can thank Mr. Eisler." Her face was flushed, and her dark brown eyes were dancing. I had to fight to stop myself from cuddling her. Mrs. Evert was more measured, and I don't think she appreciated how lucky she had been, or perhaps she was thinking about how unlucky she'd been to lose her husband.

Eisler was beaming when we returned. "Did the bank phone you, Miss Evert? Is everything to your satisfaction?"

"Thank you, Mr. Eisler. We really can't thank you enough."

"Yes," Mrs. Evert said, "it's such a relief."

"Have you canceled the radio interview?" Eisler asked.

"Of course," Georgie said. "I told the producer I'd only have good things to say, and she was no longer interested."

"Those programs are really quite disgusting. They prey on misfortune, and the last thing they want to hear is anything positive. Miss Evert, I wonder whether you might do us a small favor. We have a client who wants to check our bona fides out. His accountant heard you speaking on community radio and was worried about some of the things you said. Will you talk to him?" Eisler asked.

"Of course," Georgie smiled. "Had I known it was Ocean Cargo Containers that was responsible for realizing my father's investments, I would've never made those remarks. I have only good things to say about you and your firm, Mr. Eisler."

Eisler nodded at me. "Josh, get Mr. Denton on speakerphone."

Two minutes later Ernie Post's voice echoed around the room. "Hello, Tom," Eisler said, "we've managed to track down the young lady you've been wanting to talk to, Miss Georgina Evert. She's sitting with us and ready to answer your questions."

"And how do I know it's her?" Ernie drawled.

"Jeez, Uncle Tom, of course, it's her. What's wrong with you? You've gotta learn some trust," I yelled. "Now listen to what I–"

"I'm sorry, Tom," Eisler interrupted, "your nephew sometimes forgets himself, but he has your best interests at heart."

Then without any prompting, Georgie said, "Mr. Denton, it's

Georgie Evert. When I was on that radio program, I didn't fully understand how the container investment scheme worked, and some of the things I said were just plain wrong. Oh, and Mr. Denton, I'm staying with my mother in Sausalito. If you look up Tobias Evert in the online White Pages, you can call that number in an hour's time, and I'll answer."

"You sure'nuff sound genuine. How have you found those fellers tuh deal with? Have they been honest with you?" Ernie asked.

"They couldn't have been more helpful, and once Mr. Eisler knew what the problem was, he didn't hesitate to fix it. He was very patient and caring. As it turned out, there really wasn't a problem. It was more a misunderstanding on my part," Georgie said.

"It's a pity my nephew isn't a bit more patient."

"I don't really know him," Georgie said, "but he must be a good man. He risked his life to save my father."

"Tom, are you satisfied now?" Eisler asked.

"Almost," Ernie replied, "I want tuh talk to Miss Evert on her home line. A man can't be tuh careful these days."

"Jeez, Uncle Tom, what the–"

I never got another word out. "If you're happy after that, can we complete the transaction this afternoon?" Eisler interrupted.

"Consider it done, Simon," Ernie said.

Eisler walked Georgie and her mother to the elevators. I heard him say, "Miss Evert, do you mind calling me after you've spoken to Mr. Denton? I don't want to call him until after you've talked."

When Eisler returned to his office, he stood at the door staring at me and shaking his head. "Blackmail and shouting at your uncle. You have so much to learn. You were better before you got greedy. Forget the one hundred and twenty thousand commission. Just concentrate on closing your uncle this afternoon. Do you think you can do that, or would you like me to handle it?"

"I'm sorry. I'll be fine with my uncle."

"The worst thing you can do is to show your greed. Be nonchalant with your uncle. Let him know we have many other investors but only limited access to containers, and whatever you do, don't get angry."

I called Ernie at 3:00 p.m. and told him that he'd just made the six-million-dollar transfer to Summit, and not to answer his burner phone again today. I left it for fifteen minutes before buzzing Eisler to give him the good news. He was ebullient and was profuse with his congratulations.

I'd barely finished talking to Eisler when my cell phone rang, and Georgie's name appeared. "You were great today," she said, "I don't know what we would've done without you. Would you like to meet in the city? We could have dinner and then go to your place to watch television."

"It's not over yet, and we can't run the risk of being seen together. Don't you remember telling me that you blamed Eisler for your father's death?"

"As if I'd ever forget…. My skin was crawling today. He's such a slimy creature," Georgie said, "but there's no way he's ever going to be tried for murder."

"Don't be so sure. Who knows what I'll find out when I talk to Officer Penske?"

"When is that going to happen?"

"I don't know. I feel like I'm playing hold 'em, and I need an ace on the river to win the pot."

"What does that mean? You might as well be talking Chinese. You'll have to tell me everything tonight," Georgie said.

"It means I'm going to need some luck, and sorry, I'm going to have to take a rain check," I replied. I was already regretting my response. I didn't want to lie to her, but I didn't want to tell her what I was doing.

"What are you doing?" she asked, and then, before I could respond, she added, "Don't answer that. I trust you."

I know I should have said, 'I trust you too,' and told her what I was doing, but I also knew she would try and talk me out of it, and time wasn't on my side. "I've just got some files to tidy up, and I'm working late."

There was a pause. "You're up to something. I don't want you to take any further risks just because I said I'd like vengeance. You've already done more than enough."

"I can look after myself. Don't worry."

"All right, but are we going to catch up tomorrow night?"

"Sorry, I can't. Why don't we spend the rest of the weekend together?"

I heard her sigh. "Why don't you let me help you?"

"I'll see you on Saturday."

"Be careful. I've already lost someone I loved."

I laughed. "You're never gonna lose me."

I was the only one left in the offices at 7:00 p.m. I locked the doors and went straight to Eisler's office and opened his safe, praying that the travel agency's folder and his passport would still be there. They were. I locked the safe and hurried back to my office with his passport in hand. Thirty minutes later, I returned the folder to the safe and vacated the offices.

Chapter 31

IT WAS A BRISK 52 degrees when I left my apartment on Friday morning and, as I exhaled, little puffs of steam appeared before my eyes. I was in no hurry to get to the office and made a detour to Union Square and treated myself to a piping hot chocolate. As I left the café, I was accosted by one of the thousands of beggars who frequent the city, and he shoved a polystyrene cup in my face. He was dirty, unshaven, and stank. The sign hanging around his neck said Vietnam veteran, but he couldn't have been more than forty-five. I felt good and was looking forward to the rest of the day so I shoved two dollars in his cup and kept walking.

I entered the lobby, and our receptionist was answering a call but almost fell over herself trying to get my attention. "Mr. Eisler wants to see you immediately," she said. This was hardly unexpected, and I had to fight back a grin.

I ambled down the corridor, and Barbara greeted me with, "What have you done?"

I feigned innocence. "I'm sorry. I don't understand. What's the problem?"

Before she could answer, Eisler charged out of his office. "What's the problem? What's the problem? I'll tell you what the problem is. Your uncle's money hasn't arrived. We're out six million bucks."

"Shit! I told him to let me process the payment, but he wouldn't let me have his login details. Don't worry, he's good for it. Let me talk to him."

"I know he's good for it," Eisler said, "I've seen his bank statements, but what if he's stiffed us? What if the girl didn't stick to her part of the bargain?"

"She did. I spoke to my uncle yesterday afternoon, and he said she couldn't have spoken more highly of the firm and you personally. It's a glitch. I'll fix it. Don't worry."

"Do it now," Eisler said, shooing me down the corridor.

I couldn't help smiling on the way back to my office. Georgie's mom had her money, and I could have pulled the pin on the whole charade, but I had bigger plans for Eisler and his cronies.

By midday, the money still hadn't turned up, and I told Eisler I was having trouble with Uncle Tom. I said that he was adamant that he'd transferred the money and that he wasn't going to transfer another six million.

Eisler was in a complete panic and shouted at me, "Get him to go to the bank, and they'll be able to tell him that there's been no debit to his account. Better still, they'll be able to process the payment for him."

"I tried that. He's a stubborn old goat, and he got really annoyed with me. Said that I thought he was too stupid to know how to press a computer key."

Eisler's eyes narrowed. "You didn't get angry with him, did you? You didn't insult him, did you? I've seen how you operate when you don't get your own way."

"No and no. Look. Give me a little longer. I'll sort it out. I'll get my uncle to order a statement. If worse comes to worst we'll get the money on Monday," I said, knowing that wouldn't work for Eisler.

"I'll give you until 2:00 p.m.," Eisler said. "Then I want you in my office. This is very serious. We must have those funds today."

Later, when I walked into Eisler's office, I was stooped over, and my head was hung. My laptop was under my arm. "I'm sorry. I've tried everything. The silly old bugger knows he screwed up when he did the transfer, but he won't let me have his username and login details. I said I'd process the payment for him and he carried on something shocking. Stupid bastard!"

"Get him on the speakerphone, and I'll see what I can do," Eisler said.

I punched in Ernie's number, and he answered by saying, "Jeez, it's not you again."

Before I could say a word, Eisler said, "Tom, it's Simon Eisler. I believe there was a bit of a mix-up with your payment. Is that right?"

"Unfortunately, yes," Ernie replied. "I definitely made the transfer yesterday, but the bank's just told me it wasn't processed."

"I told you it was probably fat fingers," I said.

Eisler held his index finger up and shook it at me.

"What's fat fingers?" Ernie asked.

"It's nothing," Eisler said, "it sounds to me like your bank messed up big time, Tom. It happens, you know. We've had the same thing happen here. We process a transfer perfectly, only to have the intended recipient say he hasn't received it. It's usually the bank's fault."

"You think I should try again?" Ernie asked.

"Uncle Tom," I said, "we made commitments based on those

funds being in our account today. Mr. Eisler even leapfrogged you over some existing clients, who were really keen to increase their investments, because I'm your nephew. We know that it wasn't you who got the transfer wrong, but it'd help if we had something to show our bank."

Eisler was looking at me and silently applauding.

"Well, I'm certainly not opposed tuh that," Ernie replied. "What would you like me tuh do?"

"If you were to give me your username and login details," I said, opening my laptop, "we could print details of the transfer and email a copy to our Shanghai supplier. That would stop them from doing anything silly with the containers, like selling them to someone else."

There was a long pause with no response from Ernie.

"Tom," Eisler said, "are you there?"

"I'm thinkin'," Ernie replied, "I got over thirteen million in that account. I give you those details, and you could clean me out."

"Uncle Tom, I'm your nephew, and I'm going to be processing the transfer. I promise you it won't be for one cent more than six million. If you're worried, you should call the bank and change your username and login details as soon as the transfer is done. You don't have to though, because you can trust me."

"Simon," Ernie said, "will you make sure he doesn't do any more transfers than the six mil? Chad, just so you don't get any funny ideas, as soon as I finish this call, I'm phonin' the bank tuh change the account details."

I scowled and was about to say something when Eisler held his finger to his lips. "Consider it done, Tom. Now, why don't you give us those bank details?"

As Ernie read them out, I typed them into the PlainsCapital Bank page that I'd opened. I went to the account details, and the balance of $13,520,107.46 appeared, and I processed the transfer and watched the balance reduce to $7,520,107.46.

Eisler high fived me, and a few minutes later ended the call.

"Well done." He smiled. "You're a fast learner."

"Thanks, would you like me to call our bank and advise them to notify us on receipt of the transfer?"

Eisler laughed. "You saw the amount disappear from your uncle's account. If it's not in our account today, it will be by Monday. Don't worry about chasing our bank. I'd ask you to have a drink with me, but I'm leaving early, and I've still got a lot to get through."

As I made my way back to my office, I was pleased knowing that Eisler was relaxed and unconcerned about the six million. I guessed he was going to clean out the account from Hong Kong first thing on Monday morning. Hong Kong as a destination had puzzled me because it had an extradition treaty with the U.S. However, when I looked on the net, I saw that it had been executed while Hong Kong was still a colony of the British. China, effectively being the new owner from 1995 had no extradition treaty with the U.S., and I guessed that Eisler's friends in Shanghai had told him he had nothing to fear in Hong Kong.

At 4:30 p.m., I packed up what little personal belongings I had, including the laptop. I rationalized that for my twenty-thousand-dollar container investment, I deserved something tangible. I would not set foot in Summit's offices again.

Chapter 32

WHEN I GOT HOME, I watched the early news while making myself two toasted cheese and tomato sandwiches. I had an hour to fill before I took a cab to the airport. American Airlines 8931 direct to Hong Kong was due to depart at 9:10 p.m., but I wanted to be there no later than seven o'clock. I thought about calling Georgie, but then I'd have to lie to her again, and I hated that, so I passed. At six-thirty, I slipped my hoodie on and went outside to wait for my taxi.

The international departures terminal was buzzing, and it took me a few minutes to find the American Airlines check-in counter for flight 8931 to Hong Kong. The line for coach already stretched more than fifty yards back from the check-in counters. No one was lining up at the two counters allocated to business and first-class travelers. I reasoned that Eisler would check-in at the last possible minute, and I looked for a place where I could keep my eye on the first-class counter. Eisler had spent the past week telling me not to lose my cool and to stay calm. If he followed his own advice, my little plan would amount to nothing. I was counting on him blowing his stack.

At 8:00 p.m., I was starting to get worried. There was no sign of Eisler, and I wondered whether he'd had a change of plans. I need not have been concerned. Ten minutes later, I saw him sauntering toward the first-class check-in counter. He was wheeling a small suitcase and carrying a briefcase. I'd never seen him wearing anything other than a suit, but he looked smart in a tan suede jacket and designer jeans. He strode up to the counter, opened his travel folder, and handed his passport and ticket to the attendant. She looked up from the passport and smiled, but didn't say anything. Instead, she signaled another attendant, possibly her supervisor, and showed him the passport. I saw him shake his head before holding up the passport and showing it to Eisler. Eisler dropped his briefcase and threw his arms up in the air. He was talking rapidly and gesticulating furiously. Another attendant joined the first two, and when they showed her the passport, she shook her head vigorously. I watched Eisler thump the counter with his fist and then turn on another first-class traveler in the line behind him. I would've loved to have been close enough to hear what Eisler was saying, but his extreme body language was more than enough. Two policemen were now standing about five yards behind him, and I saw the third attendant give them the nod. They were swift and brutal, and he shouted and fought as they clamped a pair of handcuffs on him.

I jumped in a taxi at the front of the terminal and asked the cabbie to drop me in the city. I had four envelopes that I wanted to post, but I didn't want anyone to see me. I put on a thin pair of leather gloves ensuring there'd be no fingerprints on the envelopes, which were self-sealing, removing the possibility that I might be tracked down by the DNA in my saliva. The addresses were stenciled, as was the short identical memo in each envelope which said: The balances appearing on the attached bank statements represent the amounts stolen from Summit Investments by Simon Eisler and his associates. I dropped the envelopes in the post box one by one; The San Francisco Police Department, The SEC, The Justice Department, and Mr. Paul Wiese. I wasn't sure whether Wiese knew how much Eisler had salted away, but I was sure that he didn't know Eisler was going to make a run for it, and leave him to face the music. I had a feeling that he'd be more than willing to cut a deal with the prosecution for his testimony against Eisler.

I had one more envelope that I would drop into KGO-TV on Front Street on Sunday.

I was going to enjoy the final task I had to complete tonight. I hailed a taxi and told the cabbie to drop me off three blocks from Lafayette Park. It was close enough to Penske's residence.

Chapter 33

I WAS ON THE corner of Gough and Bush Streets walking slowly toward Penske's residence. As I approached, I could see Lafayette Park on the right. Penske lived in the second level of a handsome, five-level apartment building. I buzzed the front door of his apartment and got no answer. For once, luck was on my side.

I walked across the street and climbed up on the small concrete wall abutting Lafayette Park, and walked across the grass and up a slight slope until I was under a tree. I didn't know how long I would have to wait. The street light in front of Penske's building was out, and it was dark other than for occasional car lights. I was good at waiting, and the patience I'd learned as a young boy had saved my life on more than one occasion. It was cold, but nothing like what it had been in the mountains of Afghanistan. I amused myself by playing out the scenarios that might unfold in the next few days. Would Eisler be locked up or would he be successful in applying for bail? Would Paul Wiese and Barbara Sumner turn on Eisler if offered reduced sentences? Were Lanza and Selwood in on Mr. Evert's murder? The questions were many and far too hard for me to answer. I was glad my involvement would be over by tomorrow. Gough Street was peaceful, and there was little activity — the antithesis of where I lived, where fights, screaming, and bottles smashing were every night occurrences. Whether Penske owned or rented the condo was irrelevant. On his pay grade, he couldn't afford it either way. Perhaps his family were wealthy, but if that were the case, would he be a cop? I'd been in the park for over two hours, and it was nearly midnight. I hadn't thought through all the options, and it came to me that he could be sleeping over at his girlfriend's — that is, in the unlikely event that the schmuck had one. I decided to give him another hour.

Fifteen minutes later, a dark, blue Ford pulled up on the other side of the street and parked about fifty yards up from Penske's apartment building. I watched as the door opened, the interior light came on, and I saw a headful of red, cropped hair. Bingo!

I came out of the shadows and jumped down on the sidewalk. In my most timid voice I said, "Excuse me, Officer Penske, I live in the same building. Could you be so kind as to help me?"

He was on the sidewalk on the other side, and looked over at me and said, "What the hell! What is it?"

The car door was still open, and I could see him clearly now. He hadn't drawn his gun, but his hand was on the holster. "Can I have a minute of your time?" I said, nonchalantly walking toward him.

"Who are you?"

I flicked my hoodie off when I was on the sidewalk about ten yards from him. "You paid me a visit at my home. I thought I'd return the compliment. You must be doing well, living here."

"You!" he snarled, and then he smirked. "The big-time war hero who still doesn't shave. You don't scare me. What do you want?"

"I don't like getting shot at," I said, "but I was prepared to overlook it. I'm not prepared to overlook the beating you gave that defenseless journalist though."

"You're not!" He sneered, starting to advance toward me in that tough guy mode, that looks like a penguin waddling with a banana up its ass. "I'm not one of those half-starved, defenseless ragheads you killed. I'm going to enjoy giving you a bit of what that pussy Gidley-Baird got. It'll teach you to keep your nose out of things that don't concern you."

He was two yards away from me when I said, "Your condo can't be cheap. How much did you get paid to murder Tobias Evert?"

His face dropped, and I had my answer. I hadn't been certain. Now I was. Then he bellowed and charged at me swinging wild punches. I turned and ran across Gough Street and jumped up on the wall. I heard him shout, "Weak bastard. Coward," as he took off after me. I ran about fifteen yards into the park and then turned and faced him. He was like a bull, and I easily avoided him, slamming my fist repeatedly into his stomach. He was in good condition, and his abdomen was hard. I backed up the slope, parrying his punches and taking the occasional one on my arms and shoulders. I could have taken him any time I wanted to, but I didn't want to mark his face. I kept pounding his stomach and kidneys, and he dropped his arms, trying to protect his lower body. He was hurt, but still kept coming. I was throwing my punches around his arms and into his kidneys. When he tried to protect his kidneys, I attacked his stomach. It was like chopping down a tree. Besides the pain, he looked bewildered, and no doubt had expected to do to me what he had done to Gidley-Baird. By the time we reached the trees where I'd been waiting, I stopped backing away. He was hunched over trying to protect his stomach. I drove my fists deeply into his kidneys, and he grunted in agony. He'd be pissing blood for more than a week. I hadn't wanted to fight him on the sidewalk or street for fear that he might die when his head hit the ground. That was the reason I'd made him chase me into the park. I didn't have to worry. I threw a light punch to his solar plexus, and as he involuntarily straightened up, I hit him in the testicles with every ounce of power I had. He was unconscious before his head hit the grass. I bent down and checked his pulse. It was strong. Had I unloaded with the same power to his solar plexus, he may well have been dead.

I strolled down Gough Street glad that I had avenged Hamish Gidley-Baird. I had calculated what the consequences might be as soon as I'd asked Georgie to find out Penske's address. He didn't know it, but he had precious little time to do anything. He could have me arrested for assault, but that was unlikely because, other than his kidneys which would be black in the morning, he was unmarked. However, the real reason he wouldn't say or do anything officially was that he was more than thirty pounds heavier than me. I might be a 'supposed' war hero, but I looked harmless. For a thug like Penske, admitting that he took a beating from me would be nearly as bad as the beating itself.

No, he would wait until he was sure he could get away with killing me. He might hide in a high-rise building and take me out with a bullet as I walked along the street. Alternatively, he might wait in the dark near my apartment with an unmarked .38. I wasn't worried. He'd be behind bars before he had a chance to do anything.

There'd been plenty like him in the past, and I'd hoped there wouldn't be any more in the future. If he took any action, it would be via Detectives Lanza and Selwood, but, even with them, I was nearly positive that he wouldn't admit I'd beaten him up. I was now sure Penske had murdered Mr. Evert, and if Lanza and Selwood came after me, it would confirm their roles as accessories.

Chapter 34

IT WAS JUST AFTER 2:00 a.m. when I got home, and I put my phones on silent before drifting off into a heavy sleep. I woke up still feeling drowsy and lay in bed replaying the events of the previous night. It was too late to get the news on television, and I felt like a computer-free day. I wandered down to the local convenience store and bought the *San Francisco Chronicle*. I hoped there might be something in it about Eisler being detained at the airport, but I wasn't holding my breath. Imagine my surprise when I saw his photo on the front page being led away in handcuffs by the police. When I saw the photo next to it, I nearly laughed out loud. It was the first page of Eisler's passport, and the rectangular photo was enclosed in heavy black lines with thinner lines running down his face. It looked like a cell window used in the jails of yesteryear. Stenciled above Eisler's photo were the words I AM GUILTY OF FRAUD AND MURDER. The accompanying article said that Eisler had presented his passport at the airport, not knowing that it had been defaced. After unsuccessfully trying to remove the lines and words, he had become upset and abusive when he was not allowed to board his one-way flight to Hong Kong. Eisler had told the authorities that he had no idea how his passport had been defaced and that he was the victim of a malicious prank.

I remembered that my phones were still on silent, and when

I looked at my cell, there were half a dozen messages from Georgie. Instead of listening to them, I called her. Before I could get a word out, she said, "Why didn't you call me? Where have you been? Have you heard the news? I was so worried about you."

"Whoa, slow down." I laughed. "I had a late night, and I just got up. Let's not talk on the phone. I'll meet you at the bakery in an hour."

I threw on my hoodie and called a taxi.

I saw Georgie sitting at an outdoor table as the cab pulled up. I was barely out of the cab when she literally ran at me, engulfing me in a bear hug.

"I know it was you. I love you so much," she gushed. "Now tell me everything."

"Remember," I said, "you can't breathe a word of this to anyone, not even your mom." I then spent the next half hour telling her everything that had occurred.

"Why couldn't I have gone to the airport?"

"You're so cute when you pout." I teased. "It was too risky. He might have noticed us, and the game would've been up."

She punched me in the arm. "I don't pout," she said, before pausing. "Eisler paid Penske to murder my father, didn't he?"

"Yes, I'm almost certain. We'll know soon enough. If it were Eisler, he would have had to call Penske or his SFPD contact almost the minute your father went out on the ledge. There was no time for any planning, and Penske would have demanded a huge fee. If I'm right, there'll be a money trail right to his front door."

"Will Eisler go to jail?"

"Yes, he'll be imprisoned. After what I sent the government regulatory authorities, they're certain to detain him."

"Penske too?"

"Yes."

"Lanza and Selwood?"

"I don't know. Cops stick together, and they might just have been defending one of their own who they thought was getting a raw deal. They were wrong, but it doesn't mean they were in on the murder. The money trail will either bury or clear them."

"It's over, and to think you told me that you were a nothing on our first date. You're the smartest person I know."

I laughed. "If Eisler and Barbara hadn't had their little matinee that night, I would've been none the wiser. Don't confuse brains with luck."

"You're too modest," she replied, squeezing my hand tightly.

"Georgie, can I stay at your place tonight? I'm almost certain the media are going to be chasing me, and I just don't want to face them. Well, not today anyway."

She giggled. "It sounds to me like you're setting up your own matinee."

"That's not the reason, but if that's one of the offerings of the house, I'm all for it."

"Offerings of the house?" She scoffed. "I can see that you have an awful lot to learn about romance."

I had the best weekend of my life and was hoping Sunday would never end. The only love I'd ever known up until now was that of another man. I'd never forget Henry Nelson and what he had done for me, but the love I felt for Georgie was totally different. Henry had been the father I never had; Georgie was the woman I hoped to spend the rest of my life with. "This will be all over tomorrow," I said, as we cuddled on the sofa while waiting for my taxi.

"I hope so," she replied, kissing me passionately. "I love you."

"Me too."

"Me too? What does that mean?" She laughed. "Can't you say it?"

"Of course, I love you," I said. "You know that. I've said it before."

"Yes, but a girl can never hear it enough. You have so much to learn."

I was saved by the beeping of my taxi.

I asked to be dropped off a block from KGO-TV's offices. I pulled my hoodie over my head and made the short walk. A minute later I pushed the last envelope under the large glass doors.

It was midnight when I arrived home, and I didn't think the media would be waiting. I was wrong. A reporter shoved a microphone in my face and said, "It's rumored that Summit Investments is broke and that investors are going to lose millions. What do you know about it?"

"You know as much as I do," I replied, "I have no idea what's going on."

"Is that right?" A buxom woman asked, pressing her ample cleavage up against me. "Didn't you directly induce clients to invest in some sort of shipping container scheme? How can you say you know nothing?"

This was the same media that had wanted to laud me only a few short weeks ago. Now they wanted to hang me. I had to admit my conscience had taken a terrible pounding about the week I'd spent with Paul Wiese. I didn't know how much clients had invested because of me, but I felt terribly guilty. "Look," I said, "I don't have much money, but last week I put nearly every cent I had into that shipping container scheme."

"Jeez, you were conned too," one of the reporters shouted.

"They stooged their own employees," another said. "What a pack of low dogs."

Now they knew that I'd lost too, the media's questions became less offensive, and I could tell that some of them felt sorry for me. I'd always known I was going to lose the twenty thousand, but it was a small price to pay to maintain my integrity. The media no longer thought that I was involved, but they did think I was a naive fool who had been duped. I far preferred being thought of as gullible rather than crooked.

Chapter 35

I WAS UP EARLY on Monday morning, waiting for the breakfast show on KGO-TV. A weatherman was delivering the day's forecast. After finishing, he crossed to the breakfast show presenters, and I could see copies of the bank statements that I'd put in the envelope sitting on the desk between them. I had reasoned that the channel's administration would never let the contents be discussed without first taking legal advice. I had short-circuited this by marking the envelope, personal and confidential, Mr. Warren Baxter. I knew that he'd be most unlikely to let a major scoop bypass him. I was about to be proved right.

"Kathy, this story with Summit Investments just keeps growing legs. I received an envelope overnight from someone who is obviously a whistleblower, that contains the most serious allegations."

"Why don't you update viewers with the story, Warren."

"It started with a disgruntled investor, Tobias Evert, who was tragically killed while trying to get his money back. Many thought it was just the SFPD doing their job, but the whistleblower alleges he was murdered."

"Yes, a lot of people put the shooting of Mr. Evert down to his irrational actions, but there seems to be a lot more to it now. Especially after the police arrested Summit's CEO, Simon Eisler, after he kicked up a disturbance at SFO. Funny, he had a one-way ticket to Hong Kong, and it sure looks suspicious."

"He claims he was traveling to China and South East Asia with an associate from HK, and that it was easier to make the bookings there. He said he wasn't fleeing the US and had no intention of not returning."

"He actually sounded plausible, and I almost believed him." Kathy frowned, shaking her head. "I believe the shooter, who we still cannot name, was taken into custody this morning and is being questioned as we speak."

"Yes, and not only about the shooting but in relation to the savage assault inflicted on *San Francisco Chronicle* reporter, Hamish Gidley-Baird. Hamish was writing a series of articles that were highly critical of the SFPD. He's still recovering in the hospital."

"If Mr. Evert were murdered, what was the motive?"

"Kathy, our whistleblower alleges that, if Mr. Evert had lived, he would have exposed Summit's container fund as a massive Ponzi scheme."

"Yes, but what was the shooter's motive?"

"Our whistleblower alleges that, if the DA follows the money trail, he'll have the answer to that question."

"I also understand that two detectives have been suspended and are helping the DA with his inquiries. No one knows how high this could go. Perhaps the Justice Department should put a broom through the SFPD."

The cameras zeroed in on Warren Baxter. "I can reveal that the envelope we received contained copies of bank statements from international banks for amounts, which when totaled, exceed fifty million dollars. Fifty million dollars! Attached to those statements was a stenciled letter claiming that Simon Eisler and others have been milking Summit's clients for years.

We will, of course, be turning this information over to the DA, even though I've just been informed that the DA's office has also received much of the information we have, also in a stenciled envelope. Our whistleblower has obviously been busy."

"That's a sensational revelation, Warren. Rumors were rife yesterday after Eisler was arrested, and this just adds fuel to the fire of what could be some very nasty news for local investors."

"It's worse than that. Our young hero, Josh Kennelly, put his life savings into the scheme last week, and it looks like he's lost everything. What type of lowlifes fleece their own employees?"

"I want to stress it's still only speculation at this stage, and we've heard nothing from the authorities. However, it's clear that the whistleblower at Summit must hold a senior position."

"Well, he or she isn't going to be detected by their handwriting because everything in print has been stenciled."

"What should happen now, Warren?"

"Government authorities have to move quickly to get to the bottom of what appears to be a huge mess. If Mr. Evert were murdered, those responsible should spend the rest of their days in prison, but let's not forget the investors. Every effort must be made to protect them. I'm told that many senior citizens have their life savings at risk. Eisler and the other senior managers at Summit should, at a minimum, be forced to surrender their passports, and, if possible, the U.S. attorney should seek to freeze those international bank accounts. That might be easier said than done because they're all in tax havens."

"Eisler won't be traveling far on his passport, Warren." Kathy laughed.

"You're right, but I think he'll be applying for a replacement this morning. As I said, the authorities need to move quickly."

"Is there anything else they should be doing?"

"I'm speculating, Kathy, but I'd like to see arraignment proceedings commence immediately. We need to send a message to these cowboys. We have to go to a commercial now. Don't go away. We'll be back with more breaking news in a few minutes."

I was certain that Eisler wouldn't be going anywhere, and, like Warren Baxter, I wanted to see legal action commenced pronto. I was strangely tired, and I called Georgie to tell her that I'd be sleeping for the rest of the day, but that we could catch up for coffee or dinner tonight. On reflection, it wasn't strange because I'd been running on adrenalin.

I left the television on as I dozed through the day. It was dark when I woke up, and the news was on. I was still half dopey when I thought I heard the newscaster say, "Simon Eisler, Paul Wiese, and Barbara Sumner are going to be arraigned in the Superior Court tomorrow."

When I called Georgie, she told me that government investigators had virtually taken over Summit's offices. Clients had been calling all day, desperate to realize their investments. She said that several angry clients had been interviewed on talkback radio. I was surprised that she was so adamant about us attending the arraignment. "I want Eisler to know that I'm at least partially responsible for him going to prison for a long time," she said.

"He would've guessed that when the six million didn't materialize today. You don't need to go to court."

"I want to. If it were not for him, my father would still be alive today. He murdered him just as surely as if he'd pulled the trigger. He may not be charged, but I want him to know when he's doing twenty years that it's because he killed dad."

"He'll be charged," I said. "Penske's not going to take the rap by himself." I was still tired, and I sensed Georgie didn't want to come into the city. I suggested we forget about meeting up and instead catch up for coffee in the morning before walking to court.

Chapter 36

THE SKY WAS OVERCAST and most of the office workers looking for coffee or an early morning snack in Union Square were wearing overcoats. Georgie and I were sitting in a booth sipping hot chocolate and holding hands. I didn't say anything, but I wished I'd worn my hoodie. Many patrons looked over our way, and some pointed. Georgie didn't seem to notice. "I'm glad it's nearly over," she said.

I laughed. "It's not even close to over. The court cases could drag on for years."

"Perhaps," she said, "but once they're arraigned, they'll be out of action. Do you think they'll make bail?"

I turned my palms up. "I know nothing about the law or courts. I haven't got a clue."

"Sorry, I forgot that you know nothing and aren't good at anything." She smiled. "Josh, haven't you figured out that your little act doesn't work with me. I know how smart you are."

"I truly know nothing about the law," I insisted, as I helped Georgie into her chic, tan three-quarter length woolen coat. It hugged her slim body.

The court was about ten blocks away. We walked briskly to keep warm, but on the way, many people stared at me, and some were pointing. It was like Floydada again but on a far larger scale. I hated it.

Talking of Floydada, I called Ernie Post and thanked him for the mighty job that he'd done. He was as laid back as ever, but when Georgie took my cell phone to offer her thanks, he brightened up, and I could hear him laughing, even though the phone wasn't on speaker. I'd just finished saying goodbye when it started to ring. "I don't know how you did it," Lieutenant Rafter said, "but I can't thank you enough. The rats are getting cleaned out of the SFPD, all because of you."

"Thanks, Lieutenant, I didn't do much. I just got lucky."

"No one gets that lucky," he said. "Have you thought about a career in law enforcement? You're a natural."

I laughed. "Thanks, but no thanks. I don't know what I'm going to do."

"I've got some good friends in business. I could put in a word for you."

"Thanks, but I have to get my personal life sorted out before I do anything."

"You're a lucky man. She's a stunning young lady."

"Yes, she is."

"Okay. I hear you. Vicki sends her thanks. Good luck, Josh. Call me. I'd love to help you."

"Good luck, Lieutenant. I hope you make it to the top of the SFPD. You deserve to."

The gray stone court building was on the corner of McAllister and Polk and extended down both streets. The building was beveled at the intersection, and the entrance was via double glass doors. It was surrounded by angry investors, television cameras, and the media. Some of the reporters immediately made a beeline for me. Fortunately, I was not the news of the day, and there were far bigger fish to be fried. I saw a BMW pull up on Polk Street, and there was an immediate rush toward it. Paul Wiese was shaking his head and trying to push his way through the milling throng of reporters, but they weren't yielding.

I was holding Georgie's hand, and I said, "Do you want to go inside? Face it, you're not going to get close to Eisler." As I was speaking a black limousine with dark tinted windows pulled up on McAllister Street, and Eisler got out flanked by two suits. Georgie moved like lightning, and I was a good five yards behind her when I saw Eisler raise his fist like a sledgehammer. I knew I couldn't stop him, and for the first time in my life, I felt fear. Luckily, one of the suits, who was probably a lawyer grabbed Eisler's arm. Eisler snarled at Georgie and turned his back on her, but the media that had been on Polk Street were now charging toward him. I had my arm around Georgie when Eisler glanced back. His face clouded over, and he slowly shook his head.

"Do you want to watch the arraignment?" I asked.

"No," Georgie said, "he's going to jail for a long time."

"What did you say to him?"

"We set you up. There was no Tom Denton. We conned you. May you rot in hell for murdering my father."

"You were lucky that guy stopped him from hitting you."

"You mean he was lucky. He would've gotten another five years, and I'd be happy to take one punch for that," Georgie said, and a tear trickled down her cheek

I held her tightly and could feel her trembling, but it had nothing to do with the cold. I didn't have the heart to tell her that five years added to a life sentence was still life. "Let's find somewhere warm to have a drink."

"Let's go to your place." She said trying to smile.

"Fine. I'll grab a cab."

"I'd rather walk. I need to clear my head."

We walked in silence for a few minutes and then Georgie said, "You never told me about the twenty thousand. You did it to prove to them that you believed in their container scheme, didn't you?"

"Partly," I said. "I also did it because I wanted to look like I was innocent when it blew up. I feel guilty about those people who invested in the last weeks because of me. I try not to think about them.

"I'm sorry. I didn't realize you compromised your principles to get mom's money back."

"No. I compromised my principles to win a place in her daughter's heart."

"You had that from the first time we met." Georgie laughed.

"Yeah, but I didn't know it, did I?"

"Mom wanted to give you forty thousand to cover your losses, expenses and as a little reward. I told her there was no way you'd accept it."

"You were right," I agreed, "as if I could ever take money from your mother."

"I said I'd take it on your behalf. It sure swelled my bank account," Georgie said with a perfectly straight face.

I was stunned. Perhaps I didn't really know this girl. I could see her glancing at me out of the corner of her eye, and then she burst out laughing. "I told mom that it didn't matter whose account it went into. I was going to be with you for the rest of my life, and everything that I own is yours."

I started to choke up. I stopped and kissed her. "I love you," I blurted.

"Ah, now that wasn't hard, was it?" she said. "It's a shame I have to go back to New York."

For the second time in a minute, I was shocked. "I don't understand," I muttered.

This time she kept her face straight for a little longer before exploding in mirth. "I'm going back to New York on Sunday. I'm living with a couple of girls, and I have to move my stuff out and find a new place."

I must have still looked shocked. "For us," she said, "you should only need a week to get out of your apartment lease, and by that time I'll have found somewhere for us to live."

I was a little taken aback. "How do you know that I want to leave San Francisco?" I asked.

"Easy," she said. "This is such a small town. You'll always be recognized and known here. I've been watching you cringing all day. You hate it. Unless you're Donald Trump or David Letterman, you're never going to be recognized in New York. You can live in the anonymity that you crave."

She was right. "What am I going to do for a job? I'm not a lawyer, accountant, insurance agent, or a private detective. I'm a nothing."

"Here we go again." she sighed. "Don't you remember telling me you were a loner when it comes to solving problems? When we get to New York, you can throw up a sign, Josh Kennelly, Problem Solver. If it were up to me, it would be Problem Solver Supreme."

"Problem solver? You're kidding."

"No, I'm not. You could help people who've been fleeced like my dad. You're good at it. You could set up a business and do very well."

We arrived at my apartment block, and I breathed a sigh of relief to see there was no vomit on the stairs. "I've never felt fear before today," I said, "I couldn't have stopped Eisler from hitting you. Don't ever run off on me again. I love you so much."

"I love you too, Josh."

We embraced at the door for a few minutes. I was still apprehensive about her seeing the inside of my apartment. "Georgie," I said, "my apartment's a me—"

"I'm not here to look at your apartment." She smiled suggestively. "I have a problem that needs solving. Are you going to keep talking, or are you going to take me inside and solve it?"

The End

Other Books By Peter Ralph

More white-collar crime suspense thrillers
by Peter Ralph are on the drawing board.

For updates about new releases, as well as exclusive
promotions, visit the author's website and sign up for the
VIP mailing list at http://www.peterralphbooks.com/

Made in the USA
Las Vegas, NV
30 November 2020